Anonymous

The Tientsin Massacre

Anonymous

The Tientsin Massacre

ISBN/EAN: 9783337342982

Printed in Europe, USA, Canada, Australia, Japan

Cover: Foto ©Andreas Hilbeck / pixelio.**de**

More available books at **www.hansebooks.com**

THE TIENTSIN MASSACRE,

BEING DOCUMENTS PUBLISHED

IN THE

Shanghai Evening Courier,

From June 16th to Sept. 10th, 1870,

WITH AN INTRODUCTORY NARRATIVE.

SECOND EDITION.

SHANGHAI:

A. H. DE CARVALHO, PRINTER AND PUBLISHER.

THE TIENTSIN MASSACRE,

BEING DOCUMENTS PUBLISHED

IN THE

Shanghai Evening Courier,

From June 16th to Sept. 10th, 1870,

WITH AN INTRODUCTORY NARRATIVE.

SECOND EDITION.

SHANGHAI:

A. H. de Carvalho, Printer and Publisher.

THE TIENTSIN MASSACRE.

Introductory Remarks.

T is hardly an over-statement to say that the great majority of those foreigners who felt an interest in the foreign relations with China, believed that her misunderstandings and quarrels with the nations of the west were finally settled for a long time, when, in 1860, the boasted defences of her northern cities were stormed, her armies scattered like chaff, and her capital entered by foreign troops, the most sumptuous palace of her semi-deified emperor razed to the ground, and the official representatives of foreign powers established as permanent residents at his Court. But it is difficult to fathom the depths of semi-civilized duplicity, or to estimate how slow human pride and selfishness are to relinquish exclusive privileges enjoyed for ages; into what volcanic energy popular prejudice and superstition can burst when they are stirred by an agency sufficiently powerful.

For some years after the Peiho expedition had opened the way by which foreigners could, in all disputes with provincial satraps, appeal directly to the central government, there were several causes why the Chinese in their intercourse promised to prove all that foreigners expected. The stern lessons of war were still freshly remembered; the Taiping, and thereafter the Nienfei, rebellion fully tasked the energies of the ruling classes and furnished scope for all the turbulent spirits of the empire, and foreign munitions of war and active assistance were essential to the very existence of the body politic. But when the rebels were subdued; when their troops were being rapidly drilled to foreign tactics; when they saw foreign arms and vessels of war beginning to issue from their own arsenals and dockyards; when their misinterpretation and flagrant evasions of numerous rights which the Treaty of Tientsin seemed to have secured for foreigners were quietly given up by the foreign representatives: then the dearly bought lessons of 1860 began to be rapidly forgotten, and the jealousy and apprehension with which the privileged classes of China regarded the introduction of ideas and agencies calculated to overthrow their mischievous ascendency, began to show itself in many forms and places.

This uneasiness and hostility were stimulated too by the knowledge that, about the end of 1868, foreigners were entitled to claim a Revision of the Treaty, and were almost certain to demand concessions which would greatly extend their influence. The grand expedient by which, *under foreign advice*, they sought to ward off this new danger—while to well-intentioned theorists and persons of sanguine temperament it seemed admirably fitted to break down the wall of separation between China and other nations—was so conducted as to make her more haughty and exclusive than ever. For when Mr. Burlingame went forth on his mission to foreign nations, to deprecate any quickening on their part of the speed at which China was prepared to accept extended intercourse with foreigners, he bore with him a commission, and was attended by associates of a character which clearly showed to those who know the Chinese, that his mission was an embodiment of the central error of Chinese policy—the idea namely that China is the one sovereignty of the world, and that all foreign nations are her feudal dependents. And when foreign governments, ignorant of such mischievous pretensions (though well warned of their practical tendency) received the Chinese embassy with cordiality and responded to its pleas for time and forbearance

by engagements and promises that indefinitely postponed foreign improvements; the Chinese government regarded this, or
professed to regard it, as an acknowledgement on the part of
the outside nations of the deference it became them to show to
the "Middle Kingdom."

Such ideas being carefully disseminated throughout China
by the literati, a class much reverenced by the people, and
directly interested in the perpetuation of existing misgovern-
ment, it was not unnatural, however strange and unseasonable
it might appear, that while Mr. Burlingame was drawing pic-
tures as fair as they were false of China's rapid progress in all
that constitutes national improvement, the misconceptions to
which his friendly reception in Europe and America gave rise
among the Chinese, became the fruitful cause of many deplor-
able acts, which show how utterly false and misleading the
Burlingame Mission was, both in its design and in its execution.
The celebrated speech delivered by Mr. Burlingame in New
York; his successful interviews with Lord Clarendon; and
his grand reception in the centre of European diplomacy, were
fittingly succeeded by the long smouldering troubles of Formosa bursting into open violence, and were rapidly followed
by those at Chefoo, in Szechuen, at Yangchow, and Swatow.
It was supposed that such accumulated evidence of the false-
hood of Burlingame's representations would have caused a
reaction in England and America against his temporising
policy; more especially as the repressive measures of Admiral
Keppel and Consuls Medhurst, Gibson and Alabaster—men
trained under the vigorous policy of our earlier Chinese intercourse—proved in the highest degree successful. But, unhappily, Burlingame had so skilfully adapted his representations
to the favorite ideas of some leading western statesmen—ideas
which, however congenial to the condition of Europe at the
close of the nineteenth century, are as inapplicable to China
now as they would have been to Europe three centuries ago—
that he was speedily able to notify to the Chinese that England
disapproved of the action of her civil and naval officials in the

suppression of the wide-spread disturbances above alluded to.

The immediate consequence of this intimation was fresh outrages on both English and French missionaries at Nganking. These the English government speedily and without difficulty compromised for a money compensation. It was, perhaps, a significant hint of how the Chinese judged of this peaceable solution, that, when towards the close of 1869 Sir Rutherford Alcock visited Nankin, so lately the scene of Mr. Medhurst's triumph, he was subjected to an insulting slight of the Viceroy.

But other wrongs against French subjects in Kiangse and Szechuen which the Peking government was unable or unwilling to punish, determined Count Rochechouart, Chargé d'Affaires for France, to proceed up the Yangtsze in person to enforce the treaty rights of his nationals. And the firmness, energy and thoroughness with which he compelled the Viceroy Ma at Nankin to compensate the sufferers, to punish the ringleaders, and to instruct in their duty to foreigners the people at Nganking; to wring from the governor of Kiangse full indemnity for wrong done to French chapels with the cognizance of the Taotai at Kiukiang, and the pressure by which he obliged the Viceroy at Wuchang to exercise strict justice in respect of the oppressed Catholic communities of Szechuen; above all, the care he took to secure that the redress promised was actually carried into effect, had a repressive influence which can only be estimated by comparing the events of Nanking, and other places on the Yangtsze this year, with those which have recently happened at Tientsin.—[Doct. No. 1.]

But among the retributive measures which Rochechouart enforced during his visit to the Yangtsze was the degradation of an officer who was proved to have been an active instigator of the wrongs done to the French missionaries, their converts and property. Probably the Count did not know how thoroughly he had earned his punishment. For that officer was Cheng-Kwo-Shwai, a short account of whose antecedents, character, influence and connection with the recent and existing troubles at Tientsin and Peking will be found in Nos. 41, 8, 9, 10, 35,

53, 60, 68, 74, 75 and 78 of the accompanyiug documents. From these it will be seen that his life has been devoted, with all the energy of a fearless and enthusiastic temperameut, with all the stern fixity of purpose to be derived from an inherited vow, to the expulsion of foreigners from China. His degradation by Rochechouart lashed his ruling passion into ungovernable fury, the more intense because it now became concentrated against the French. And this concentration, too, assisted him in giving it expression in action; for it would be easier to induce the Chinese to attack one foreign power than all combined, and the more definite the object of attack, the more exactly could he fit his machinery to the work to be done.

The circumstances of the case were not unfavorable. Burlingame was dead, and his death must have weakened the honestly pro-foreign party of Chinese politicians (if there were any such), who hoped, through him, to introduce foreign improvements with a gradualness which would obviate social convulsions. His death, too, made it unnecessary if not impossible for the anti-foreign party to wear any longer the mask which the maintenance of his mission involved. England and America had shown how strongly disinclined they were to mingle unnecessarily in the wars of China. Political and religious differences seemed likely to prevent any cordial co-operation between Russia and France. Germany has never had occasion to impress China with any idea of her power. France was isolated. Her military prestige has suffered a serious blow in the eyes of the Chinese by her expedition to the Corea. She alone had failed to give the Chinese embassy any assurances of co-operation and had in consequence got something like a menace from Burlingame; a fact of which the Chinese have doubtless been made aware. The political training, experience and associates of Cheng-Kwo-Shwai warrant us in believing that he was fully able to appreciate these various aspects of the position of France in reference to China. But there were other aspects of the actual position of the great

bulk of French subjects in China, the value of which as a basis
for inaugurating a national attack against them, this practised
agitator has, by his subsequent conduct, only too clearly shown
how thoroughly he understood. These aspects may be regarded
as fourfold :—

1. The judicial and administrative system of China is so
corrupt that the western nations, in making treaties with her,
could not consent, as they do among themselves, that their
subjects, when residing in China, should be judged by Chinese
law administered by Chinese judges. They, therefore, availed
themselves of the international expedient of extra-territorial
jurisdiction, according to which foreigners in China committing wrong are amenable only to officers of their own several
nationalities. France claims to protect all ecclesiastical persons of the Roman Catholic church as her nationals. Wherever, therefore, a Catholic priest is found in China, he is
independent of the local authorities. This makes him a person
of considerable importance. Foreign treaties also guarantee
that no Chinese subject shall be molested by the Chinese
magistrates for becoming a Christian, and it naturally falls to
the foreign priest to see that his converts have the full benefit
of this proviso: and this priest having direct access, through
the French minister at Peking, to the central government, the
provincial magistrates dare not openly set his interference at
naught. When to these considerations is added that reverence
which the converts would naturally feel for their religious
instructor, it can be readily understood how willingly, in all
their difficulties and disputes, they would have recourse to the
house of the priest rather than to the yamên of the mandarin,
especially when, instead of the oppressive exactions of the latter
(which make a Chinaman fear a magistrate almost as much as
a robber), they found that their disputes were settled, and
their wrongs redressed with disinterested justice and without
expense. But it will also be easily understood how such a
desertion of the yamêns would move the bitter jealousy and
hostility of the mandarins, and how eagerly they would en-

deavour to decry those who were not going beyond the plain duty of Christian priests, as the meddling partisans of a grasping foreign power.

2. One of the most beneficent and persuasive means by which foreign missionaries have sought to commend Christiannity to the acceptance of the Chinese has been by dispensing among them the benefits of western medical science. But in the Chinese pharmacopœia, parts of the human body are largely made use of as ingredients, and the more mysterious or vital the organ so made use of, the more does the drug compounded from it seem to be regarded as efficacious to secure the object for which it is used; and Chinese medical knowledge being much in the same state as it was among western nations two or three hundred years ago, it deals largely in charms, philtres, potions, spells, and other magical absurdities. It may be doubted whether the horrible substances referred to are actually used, but it is an undoubted fact that Chinese books say so, and that the Chinese believe they are so used. It thus becomes easy to understand how simple a task it must be to persuade an ignorant and prejudiced people that foreign doctors make use of similar drugs for similar purposes—all the more so because they are known to practice anatomy and surgery, which are abhorrent to the Chinese mind.

3. Kidnapping of children has from the earliest historic times been prevalent in China; and the various Foreign and Mixed Courts established in China have made it indisputable that the practice is still of daily occurrence. Female children so kidnapped are sold to brothels which, in fact, are mostly replenished from this source, while male children are sold as slaves or are bought for adoption by childless persons. Now the Catholic missionaries have always devoted special attention to the young in China; their peculiar view of the efficacy of infant baptism, their sagacious appreciation of the ultimate influence of educating the young, and the large number of children (especially females) exposed in China by poor parents, all combined to give this direction to their efforts. For the

reception of these children they have erected capacious Orphanages and Industrial schools in many parts of China. It is not difficult to see how among a people to whom kidnapping is familiar and who are prejudiced against foreigners, the sight of large numbers of children collected by foreigners in their establishments, could be easily made the ground of a charge that they were gathered together by nefarious means and for unholy purposes.

4. The whole life and object of a religious missionary cannot fail to be utterly incomprehensible to a people whose entire range of ideas is to a marked degree, of a secular and materialistic type. And in the case of the Catholic missionaries this mystery is intensified by the air of solemnity and secresy which their impressive style of worship, and such religious exercises as Confession, throw over their whole procedure. This remark applies with special force to their Seminaries, where a considerable degree of seclusion is almost unavoidable.

Those who have read the account of the Szechuen troubles published in the *North China Daily News* of December 1869. and who will read Document No. 51 of the present series, will observe what an effective use has been made of the first of the four aspects of Catholic missionary operations above enumerated, in fanning into a flame the anti-foreign spirit of China. But it was by a most skilful and masterly combination of the last three aspects that Cheng-Kwo-Shwai succeeded, during the past summer, in stirring up an intense anti-foreign and especially anti-French excitement along the whole lower valley of the Yangtse, from the heart of Szechuen and Hunan to the Yellow Sea; an excitement which first assumed a threatening form around and in Nanking (Document No. 1), but being there repressed, was raised to the point of explosion by the arch-agitator on his way northwards through Shantung and Chihli, till, a few days after his arrival, and under his personal leadership, it found a first, and fitting, but let us also hope a final, culmination in the Tientsin massacre of the 21st of June.

All the offended pride and disappointed selfishness and awakened jealousies of the officials; all the fears of a superstitious people, and the deepest seated and most universal of human instincts were appealed to against foreigners, but more especially against those whose plan of working seemed most liable to suspicion. The appeal was made by means of those way-side placards which in China form a miserable substitute for the newspaper press of western nations, and combine in a wonderful degree the minimum of its benefits with the maximum of its abuses. These, diffused with organized diligence and universality, from the frontiers of Kweichow to beyond Peking, told the masses of China that foreign missionaries abetted and subsidized a system of kidnapping throughout the empire; that by means of devilish medicines supplied to abandoned wretches, they exercised such a magical influence over children that they willingly followed them, though utter strangers; that by these scoundrels they were handed over to the missionaries, who collected them in their establishments and slaughtered them in secret, for the purpose of using their eyes and hearts and private parts for the manufacture of their abominable drugs.

Great as was the popular excitement produced by such foul calumnies, it was fomented and legitimised by the timidity or stupidity of some mandarins, and the guilty complicity of others, from the Viceroy downwards to common village magistrates. For the officials everywhere issued proclamations announcing that the kidnappers were abroad, offering rewards for their detection, and insinuating more or less distinctly that they were the paid emissaries of foreigners. The popular fury thus called forth demanded some victims, and these a cowardly, time-serving magistracy were bound to find. The result was that at Nanking no less than eighteen alleged kidnappers were beheaded in one day. On what kind of evidence these men were condemned may be guessed from what is said of the two executed by the Che-fu of Tientsin (Doct. 8) in whose case even the literati felt called on to protest against the irregularity of the proceedings.   Such executions rather excited than satisfied the popular thirst for vengeance, and they were easily excited by the secret instigators and directors of the movement to invoke vengeance on the more guilty heads of the alleged paymasters of the kidnappers.   The result may be seen in the "Nanking Tumults" described in Document No. 1.

But the Catholic clergy made an appeal to Ma, the Viceroy, too direct and explicit to enable him to shirk the subsequent responsibility if mischief befell them.   Besides, he could not so soon forget the severe lessons taught him by Medhurst, at the end of 1868, and by Rochechouart at the end of 1869.   He was forced to take energetic steps; and as surely as he did so, the tumult was effectually quelled.   The arch-agitator Cheng-Kwo-Shwai meanwhile, without awaiting results in the valley of the Yangtse, proceeded to fire his train, already laid, in some place where favorable influences might develope it into an effectual conflagration.   From his residence at Yangchow, whence, as from a centre, he had for years spread out in all directions the network of his machinations, he directed his course to the metropolitan province of Chihli.   Various considerations may have determined this destination.   It is the centre of official interest and cabal; it is under the government of his powerful friend Tsêng-Kwo-Fan, the reputed head of the anti-foreign party in China.   At Tientsin is the grave of his great foster-father San-Ko-Lin-Sin, a visit to whose tomb formed a specious pretext for his journey.   With Taku forts greatly strengthened from what they were in 1860, and wanting only men, according to Chinese notions, to make impregnable; with a large force of foreign drilled troops, and a foreign arsenal and powder-mill close at hand; with large establishments of the hated Catholics both at Tientsin and Peking, and doubtless also with the knowledge that under such a Governor-General the local magistrates would be willing tools for this work, we cannot wonder that Cheng-Kwo-Shwai directed his journey northwards.

He had indeed prepared his way before-hand.   The accompanying documents (Nos. 8, 9, 10 and 12) show how a month before his arrival the cry of kidnappers had arisen; how the Che-fu had executed his victims, issued his incendiary proclamation, and received the complimentary umbrella and tablets from the grateful abettors of the anti-foreign system; and how, all over the country, between Tientsin and Yangchow, as far as foreign observation reached, (nearly 200 miles), the country was filled with announcements of the impending doom of the foreigners, and more particularly of the French at Tientsin.

It should be noticed that while the general substance of the placards was everywhere the same, they were skilfully varied to hit the peculiarities of different localities. At Nanking attention was called to the size of the vaults beneath the Catholic premises, and the underbuilding, which was really intended to afford healthful drainage and ventilation, was alleged to be devoted to the most fiendish purposes. At Tientsin the same skill in giving intensity to the general charges by calling in the aid of local purposes was shown by the use that was made of the transference of some coffins from an old burying ground to the cemetery surrounding the French cathedral. We are sorry that our having failed to obtain any authenticated copy of the placards diffused by Cheng-Kwo-Shwai along his journey northward, prevents us from saying positively whether the same adaptation to local peculiarities was observed in all his incendiary effusions. What we do know is, that the popular excitement which marked his progress indicated his route as by a streak of fire.

At length on the 18th June the whole aspect of things became so alarming; the offensive proclamation of the che-fu had so excited the people, and the warnings of friendly natives assumed such definiteness and consistency, that H. B. M.'s Consul Mr. W. H. Lay felt called on to draw the attention of Chung-How to the state of affairs. Chung-How is a man of all but the highest rank, who, as superintendent of the northern ports, has the supreme control of Tientsin and its neighbourhood, a post he has held since the close of the last war. (Document 48.) He sent no reply to Mr. Lay's representation of the 18th.

Allowing Sunday, the 19th, to pass Mr. Lay again wrote on the 20th still more urgently, requesting Chung-How's interference. This also remained unanswered, as was another similar communication sent on the morning of the 21st, when the crowds were already assembling for their work of blood. (Document No. 2.) And be it here remarked that, amid all the light which subsequent proceedings have cast on these transactions while it has been again and again repeated that all the foreign ministers have exculpated Chung-How of all guilty connection with the massacre, we have not yet seen any explanation of his failing to answer Mr. Lay's repeated warnings and remonstrances. On the other hand, and in contradiction to an attempt made to prove that the defection of his troops had rendered him powerless, (Document 48) it is distinctly stated that when he interfered to keep the rioters from extending their attack to the foreign settlement, his interference was successful (Document No. 8).

In Document No. 50 it will be observed that an attempt is is made by the Chinese authorities to represent the massacre at Tientsin as the result of a mob, collected by rumours of kidnapping at the Catholic establishments, and excited to open violence by the imprudent discharge of a weapon by the French Consul. To this view of the case we oppose a statement of well ascertained facts, which will be found narrated in detail in the various documents referred to. It was known hundreds of miles round Tientsin, as far south as Tsinanfoo the capital of the province of Shantung, that foreigners and especially the French *were to be attacked* on the 21st June. (Document 8.) On the morning of the massacre the fire guilds went in from Pukow, 35 *li* (12 miles) from Tientsin *to be in time* for the massacre, and the same is said of other places within a 40 *li* radius. The attack was not made by a promiscuous mob assembled at random, but by two well known organised bodies, the fire guilds and the volunteers, whose leaders are members of the ruling class, (Literati) their names being regularly enrolled in the court of the city magistrate.

And the fact that the firemen were equipped, not as usual with buckets, but with fighting weapons, and that they were summoned to and recalled from the attack by the regular official call, show indisputably that the attack was premeditated and organised (Document 8 and 12). Further, the attack was not commenced by the French Consul firing a pistol. The evidence of documents Nos. 2, 8 and 12 shows that the first blood-shed took place at the French Consulate during Fontanier's absence trying to obtain assistance from Chung-How. The number of yamen runners too who were observed among the rioters, (Document 28) the fact that the auxiliaries who came to the attack from the east of the river were lead on and encouraged by well known high military officers, (Document 8) and the statement borne out by the fans, on which the massacre has since been depicted, that the che-fu was present and saw the destruction of the Consulate and Cathedral (Doct. No. 8), all show how completely the native magistracy were implicated in the occurrence.

What followed when the slaughter was fairly commenced, it is sad to follow out in all its ghastly detail; how Monsieur and Madame Thomassin, a newly married pair *en route* from Paris to the Legation at Peking, fell under many wounds in the French Consulate during the Consul's absence, the priest Chevrier and his attendants speedily sharing the same fate; how the Consul after having been repeatedly at Chung-How's yamên, finally went there again at 2 P. M. accompanied by his chancellor M. Simon in his official dress and armed, how his appeals to Chung-How were unheeded and he was dismissed by that official with insult; how, as it would seem in the very precincts of the yamên, they were forced to use their weapons in self defence; how in a wounded state they tried to push on for the Consulate till they were literally cut to pieces by the raging crowd; how Monsieur and Madame Chalmaison living within the native city were attacked almost at the same time, and how when the lady having first escaped was impelled by natural affection to seek for her husband's corpse under cover of the succeeding night, she was seized and ruthlessly butchered; how to the east of the river a Russian gentleman with his wife married four days previously, and a friend, were assaulted in their chairs, and though they used the plea that they were English were slain without mercy, the lady being also exposed to brutal indignities; how the crowd having finished their work of blood and fire at the Consulate and Cathedral made for the Hospital of the Sisters of Mercy, situated half a mile off and were joined by a number of fire guilds from the east of the river; how the noble ladies used every means to disarm their fury, and finding all means useless begged them at least to spare their Chinese converts; how they were insulted, stripped, impaled, ripped open, cut to pieces, thrown into heaps and made so that out of nine only four bodies have been received, and of these most have been mere unrecognisable fragments; how as a fit accompanyment to the rest, 30 or 40 of the children of the Hospital were smothered in the vaults where they had taken refuge, while a still larger number of older persons were carried away to the prisons of the city to be there subjected to tortures of which they bore such terrible evidence when their release was at length effected (Documents 2, 8, 10, 12, 25, 28, 32, 36, 39, 42, 45 and 56).

From evidence given in Document 28 it will be seen, that the instigators of these outrages prepared the minds of their tools gradually, till they were at last worked up to the requisite pitch of fanaticism. And it seems to have been intended by some of them that the destruction of the French would be the signal for a descent on the foreign settlement, while the minds of the populace were still excited. But if this were the intention, it miscarried. There seemed to be a widespread understanding that the attack on the Settlement was to be deferred to the 24th June. As it was, 200 men attempted to make a raid into the Settlement; but the authority of Chung-How, and of the che-hsien were exerted to prevent it, (Document 8). It is also said that some shopkeepers friendly to foreigners damped the ardour of the rioters (Document 32). The delay thus gained enabled the foreigners in the Settlement to take such measures for defence as sufficed so keep the enemy at bay till gun-boats enough arrived to put an end to all hazard of an immediate attack. But wherever foreign property could be reached it was attacked and destroyed. Thus 8 Protestant and 8 Roman Catholics chapels were destroyed, while the converts of both all over the country have been subjected to personal outrage and spoliation. It does not excite surprise to learn in these circumstances that such foreigners as happened to be in the country round Tientsin made their escape with great difficulty, it being found necessary to send a guard for one of them (Document 36).

The condition of the bodies as they were recovered is detailed in document No. 2, where there will also be found a singular instance of Chung-How's attemps at mystification throughout this whole affair. H. B. M.'s Consul, Mr. Lay, having been requested to act as French Consul in room of the deceased Fontanier, it thus fell to him to see to the burial of the thirteen bodied that were recovered, which were interred in the English Cemetery provisionally till their ultimate disposal should be decided on by Count Rochechouart. Funeral services in honour of the dead were held in most of the foreign communities in China. An account of that held in Shanghai will be found in Document 18. The universal sentiment of grief and indignation felt by foreigners of all nations was also well expressed by many addresses of condolence of which specimens will be found in Documents 15, 16 and 17.

The news of the massacre naturally excited the fears of foreigners at the different ports, encouraged unfriendly manifestations on the part of the unruly and has disquieted the minds even of the peaceable by ever varying rumours. Thus from Peking (Docts. 10, 14, 53, &c.), from Chinkiang (19 and 40), from Newchwang (27), from Chefoo (13) and from Ningpo (73) there are rumours tending to keep people's minds in an uncomfortable and unsettled state.

In the case of the river ports Chinkiang, Kiukiang and Han-kow, a certain amount of confidence has been restored by the presence at each of a British gun-boat, and at Shanghai, Chefoo and Tientsin naval assistance has been supplemented by the organisation of a Volunteer force, that of Shanghai numbering over 600 men, though that is of course by far the largest. The force is under the control of the Municipal Council (Doct. 30).

Immediately on the news from Tientsin arriving all eyes were naturally turned to Peking to see what action would be taken by the Foreign Ministers. It is understood that some delay occurred in getting authentic news of the massacre to Peking, so that telegraphic news does not seem to have been forwarded to Europe till the 26th July. But even that message seems to have been delayed by a series of unfortunate and most suspicious accidents, so that while private telegrams have gone safely and been duly replied to, this a matter of the deepest interest and importance to so many different nations, does not seem as yet to have elicited a reply.

At Peking all seems uncertainty: the English speaking Legations, representing by far the greater number of foreigners in China give no sign of any policy; while already the American missionaries at Tungchow have been forced to seek for safety under the protection of British guns at Chefoo, and families are preparing to migrate from Peking, Tientsin and Newchwang.

The assassination of the Viceroy Ma at Nanking on the 23rd August which is said to be an act of vengeance for the part he took in behalf of foreigners in the troubles of June (although this is disputed) adds another element of disturbance and apprenension to the minds both of natives and foreigners (Document 70). In connexion with this, too, we have fluctuating, yet on the whole consistent, accounts of the concentration of 100,000 troops within a day's journey of Tientsin, while five of the most distinguished generals have been summoned from all parts of the empire to the same centre of operations.

Meanwhile what are the Ministers doing? Nothing as yet. That they should delay taking action till they saw what the

Chinese Government proposed to do was only reasonable. But when Tsêng-Kwo-Fan, the commissioner appointed by the Chinese Government, has reported that foreigners are forsooth innocent of kidnapping, and that those who killed the foreigners should be punished; while now at the end of 3 months no effort is made to seize the guilty, and a decided and contemptuous refusal is given to the request that the chief and well known criminals should be brought to justice, surely it is high time that some decided policy should be adopted. The unhappy complications which have arisen in Europe may for a time paralyse the action of Count Rochechouart, but England, America and Russia are free to act and are incurring a heavy, it may be a fatal, responsibility in keeping both Chinese and foreigners longer in suspense.

No. 1.

THE NANKIN TUMULT.

June 16th, 1870.

The disturbance at Nankin threatens to be one of the most serious that has yet occurred in connection with the residence of foreigners in the interior. As yet the history of the movement is not accurately known, for the excitement prevailing in the city prevents the transmission of authentic information. But the general character of the tumult is tolerably well understood. A cry is set up that certain infamous people are engaged in kidnapping children, not an uncommon practice, and therefore, not at all incredible. Such rumours are born and die a hundred times without exciting public attention, and so it might have happened in the present case, but for what appears to have been the indiscreet conduct of the city authorities at Nankin. Instead of ignoring the foolish rumour, or issuing proclamations forbidding its spread, the civic dignataries seem to have entered most fully into the spirit of it. They might, indeed, for some occult purpose have been feigning alarm, while they worked on the popular frenzy; or they might have been sincerely overcome by the panic of the moment; but the action they took was of all things the most calculated to fan the smoking fire into a flame. Proclamations were issued offering rewards of 100 dollars for the apprehension of the kidnappers. By this means of course all lingering doubts were dispelled; and the populace thus forcibly convinced of the reality of the alleged crimes, became excited to an extraordinary degree. The authorities appear to have lost their heads, and in their attempt to allay the tumult which they have done so much to create, they have only made matters worse and worse. People were arrested in the street on suspicion, and no stranger could safely shew himself in public for fear of being immediately thrown into prison. When the affair had grown to this extent it began to take on a new phase, and the cry spread like wild-fire, that the foreigners were the culprits for whom the people were in search. It would only be a conjecture to say that in this, as in all other similar cases, it was the mandarins and literati who gave this particular direction to the popular clamour, but if they did, they soon found that they had raised a spirit which they could not control. The only foreigners in Nankin are French and English missionaries; and they were immediately besieged by the howling mob, and menaced in person and property. Mr. Hudson Taylor, late of Yangchow, mindful of the retreating attitude of the British government, and of the distinct advice of Lord Clarendon to run away from danger; conscious also, no doubt, that if he by remaining in Nankin became the hero of another disturbance, he might not only become a martyr, but be afterwards held up to the execration of the English public by the *Times* and its following, ordered his party away from the city. The French missionaries and their congregations were thus left to bear the whole brunt of the storm. Their houses were carefully searched by the mandarins, and no limbs of kidnapped bodies were found lying about the neat little whitewashed rooms of the missionaries or their neophytes. But it appeared as if all attempts to satisfy the mob only goaded them to further excesses; and the mandarins now found it necessary to put their prisoners to the torture in order to get confessions out of them. Under this cruel process a number of them actually confessed to having kidnapped children at the instigation of foreigners. These poor wretches were beheaded for the gratification of the mob—some accounts say to the number of seventeen—and among them at least one Christian. Everything having been thus done, wittingly or unwittingly, to stimulate the popular hostility to foreigners, the last accounts that have reached us from the city are to the effect that the French missionaries are in hourly expectation of being attacked and pillaged, if not killed. It is needless to say that this is not a contingency which the authorities contemplate with satisfaction. With Yangchow, Nankin and Nanchang so fresh in his memory, the Vice-roy is not likely to provoke another quarrel with foreigners; and he has accordingly issued proclamations defending the foreigners from the absurd allegations that have been worked up against them. This tardy measure of the Vice-roy's seems however to be as yet without effect.

The peculiarity of the present excitement is, that it has spread into every part of the province, and may produce a dangerous outbreak at any point. Yangchow, Chinkiang and Tanyang, and doubtless other cities from which we have no exact information, are in a ferment; vague but horrible suspicions about foreigners have taken possession of the minds of the ignorant people everywhere, and as a story does not lose in the telling, even the monstrous accusations of Nankin are probably found in an exaggerated form in the distant cities.

This unfortunate affair will probably be used in argument by those who maintain that there is a danger to the public peace in admitting foreigners into the interior of China; for here, it will be said, the demonstration is entirely spontaneous on the part of of the people and the authorities have been powerless to keep down the excitement. The latter has undoubtedly been shewn to be true, but it still remains to be proved that the authorities had no share in instigating the affair, or, at all events, in directing it against the foreigners. It may be said also that merchants would never be likely to attract the hostility of a Chinese mob, at least not for any any such chimera as has moved the populace of Nankin, for a merchant's motives are perfectly intelligible to the Chinese. It is different with a missionary. He is an utterly incomprehensible man to the Chinese; his motives are to them unfathomable, and there is, consequently, nothing too extravagant for them to believe about him. One of his objects is to collect children about him and teach them gratuitously, if he does not even pay them for coming to him. Why an intelligent man should forsake his country and his kindred, and travel over sea and land to do that, will perhaps always remain a puzzle to the Chinese. Nor is it to be much wondered at, that when questions of kidnapping children crop up, the well known habits of the missionary should expose him to the most absurd suspicions. Were the missionaries known to levy black-mail on the Chinese, they would probably inspire more confidence, by supplying the natives with a rational theory of their existence.

<hr />

No. 2.

THE TIENTSIN MASSACRE.

(From our Correspondent.)

TIENTSIN, *22nd to 27th June*, 1870.

The account given in the *Evening Courier* of June 16th, of proceedings at Nankin, would be an accurate description of the preliminary part of our troubles here connected with missionary matters; the same story of kidnapping children, of the missionaries purchasing them and taking out their eyes for medicine, &c., the same knowledge of the authorities of what was going on, the same (apparent) indifference on their part to the probable consequences, were conspicuously displayed here some time before the massacre. Threatenings of this kind had become so frequent that to a certain extent, they came to be treated like the cry of Wolf! Wolf! in the fable, so that when the sad reality did come, no one was prepared. The first intimation we had of trouble to our friends in the city was the sight of fire, which proved to be caused by the burning of the French cathedral and consulate adjoining, and the premises of the Sisters of Mercy, some half mile nearer the Settlement. Almost immediately after, news reached us of the murder of three foreigners; and, a little later, we heard of the terrible deaths of no less than fifteen to eighteen foreigners, all of whom were French, and including the consul, Fontanier; M. and Madame Thomasin who had only arrived a day or two before *en route* for Peking; the chancelier, M. Simon; a Jesuit father, M. Chevrier, and, saddest of all, the poor Sisters of Mercy, nine in number. To them indeed no mercy was shown: the cruel outrages upon them are horrible even to relate; their clothes are said to have been torn off them, their bodies stabbed and ripped open, their breasts cut off, and their eyes dug out. To crown all, the Chinese report this morning that all that is left of them are two charred masses, some distance apart, and quite impossible to be recognised. Truly a crown of martyrdom have they received from the ungrateful people in whose service, and for whose welfare, their lives were being spent here. M. and Madame Chalmaison, French, are also said to have been killed while attempting to reach the foreign settlement. Three Russian subjects, Mr. and Mrs. Protopopoff and Mr. Basoff met with the same fate on the other side of the river close to the salt-stacks which are near the foreign settlement. The above took place about 2 o'clock on the afternoon of the 21st. To show that the attack was premeditated and threatened, I may mention that my workmen two miles or more from the scene of action said to me on seeing the fire that Englishmen had nothing to fear, for the attack was only on the French. Whether the Chinese apprehended immediate retribution or not, I cannot say, but hardly a man was to be seen in the settlement after the first fire took place; on the following day labour was partially resumed.

22nd.   To-day H. E. Chung-How met the consuls at the house of the commissioner of customs.   He seemed bewildered, and intimated that the day's work had made him a poor man, and that he would now be responsible for the lives of foreigners; at the same time he offered to send down a guard of six hundred soldiers.   But the British consul strongly objected to any such step, while another gentleman, a consul for more than one treaty power, and at the same time occupying the anomalous position of paid servant of His Excellency, was for leaving everything *as in duty bound* to His Excellency!   The foreign residents from the first took steps to protect themselves, and during the last two nights have kept watch and guard.   The *Manchu* was fortunately here, and by the kindness of her agent and captain, was a refuge for all who might require it, and is to remain here until another steamer of the same Company arrives.   The *Appin* also arrived here to-day; so that if an attack on the Settlement takes place, the two steamers could protect all foreigners.   The *Dragon* left Taku on the morning of the 22nd with the *Racer*, a dismasted vessel, in tow and with news of the attack here which overtook her at Taku, together with a request from the British consul for the *Opossum* gun-boat to come on here from Chefoo.

This morning early, three foreigners, Mr. Cox, British, and Messrs. Cordes and Perizot, North-German subjects, came down to the Settlement from the city.   This morning also a Chinaman was found in the steeple or tower of the Protestant church built on mission ground, close to the Settlement, with balls of combustible materials for the apparent purpose of firing the church.   During the day a Chinaman in the Settlement was found with a revolver up his sleeve, who finding he was being caught, succeeded in throwing the weapon into the river.   Both these Chinese have been handed to the native authorities.

23rd.—This morning there was found in the river, quite fresh, the bodies of the two Russians before named, man and wife, whose wedding had been celebrated less than a week ago amid great rejoicings.   The bodies were stripped, and the young wife, only about 16, had her arm broken and cuts on face and body, and three fingers cut off, apparently for the sake of the rings.   The freshness of these bodies is supposed to be due to their contact with the salt-stacks where they were killed.   They had only been a short time in the water.   Another body found at the same time could not be recognised, and is believed to be Chinese.   Since then a fourth body found in the water horribly cut about the head and face, and with part of one hand cut off, was recognised by two French subjects, Messrs. Borel (2) and Courtraix, who have made their escape from the city, as being the body of the French consul, M. Fontanier; his socks also bore the initials H.F. This body was also stripped; at the time he met his death he wore the consular uniform. Yesterday H. E. Chung-How said the consul's body was one of seven taken out of the water and put in coffins. These bodies are to be kept until the arrival of the French authorities from Peking, expected here to-day or to-morrow. Mr. and Mrs. Staminan, and Mr. Meyer, came down to the Settlement this morning under an escort from Chung-How; they are believed to be the sole survivors of the foreigners who were in the city; twenty or twenty-one are dead or missing, and of these, twelve are women—nine sisters, Mrs. Thomasin, Mrs. Chalmaison, French, and Mrs. Protopopoff, Russian.

It appears the French consul, on the attack being made, had gone to Chung-How's yamên, and induced Chung-How to accompany him to the consulate. On their way thither they met the che-hsien, and Chung-How's story is that the consul fired at the che-hsien, whereupon the mob rose and cut him down, killing him on the spot. Mr. and Mrs. Thomasin were killed inside the consulate. Mrs. Chalmaison got on her horse and escaped, her husband being killed in his door-way as he was coming out. Mrs. Chalmaison returned to the house in the evening in Chinese dress, but it seems the omission to change her foreign boots led to her detection, and she was slaughtered in the street.

Full particulars of these transactions may never be known, but already a good deal of light is thrown on the affair from various quarters. We hear from a distance in the country of ten days' journey that proclamations were up against Catholics on account of their malpractices; but as the people could not discriminate between Catholic and Protestant, they were advised to take them all to the yamên for examination.

One of Tsêng-Kwo-Fan's lieutenants is now here with an escort of 80 to 100 troops, with no ostensible object. It is somewhat curious that when Tsêng-Kwo-Fan himself was down here last year, one of the rumours accounting for his visit was his intention to seize the French consulate, it being imperial property; and it is also note-worthy that when some of us in 1861 endeavoured to purchase this same property, we were told it could not be sold, as it belonged to the emperor.

24th.—The two Russian bodies were buried in the British cemetery yesterday afternoon, and shortly after, the body of the third Russian was found in the river, and was buried this morning. Yesterday the Chinese authorities sent down to the British consulate five coffins containing bodies which were recognised as those of Mr. and Mrs. Thomasin of the French legation, M. Simon of the consulate, Father Chevrier and a Chinese priest. M. Simon was so hacked as to be hardly recognisable. Mrs. Thomasin was cut in the back of the neck. She had her clothes on. These bodies with the French consul's, six in number, have all been placed to-day in the British cemetery, pending instructions from the French authorities, as it was impossible to keep them above ground any longer.

Reports this evening are to the effect that Tsêng-Kwo-Fan is now on his way down here with 5,000 troops to investigate into this sad affair. Despatches from the North-German consul for Peking had been stopped and returned to the consul, his courier had been taken to the magistrate in the city and bambooed; but a despatch from the British consul to the minister had reached Peking, and an answer from Mr. Adkins received here last night. At the same time came letters from the French minister asking for further particulars, having heard of the death of the consul and others. All was quiet in Peking. The attempt of the authorities to interrupt communication between officials at Peking and Tientsin is however a suspicious circumstance.

On the 24th the body of a Chinese woman was found in the river; by the ornaments about her neck she was a Catholic, and believed to have been a teacher in the Sisters' school. She. was much cut and disfigured; the body was buried with the other six.

26th.—This morning six coffins were sent down from the city, the contents of which on examination proved to be, the bodies of Mr. and Mrs. Chalmaison; of the remaining four, two contained bodies half burnt, one of which had evidently been in the water and had apparently been partially eaten; the second was in much the same horrible state; the remaining two were burnt to a cinder; in one, only the scull and a few bones remained. I forced myself to look upon these six, and hope I may never see such another sight. Whether the four were the remains of Sisters or of Chinese it is impossible to say. The six coffins were placed side by side with the other seven, one large mound covering the whole thirteen coffins. The Chinese who brought them said the four were Sisters; they lay close to the gates, first one, then two, then one; there were also Chinese bodies there which they had instructions not to touch; but there were no other foreign bodies there.

27th.—Word has been sent down to the effect that no more foreign bodies are to be found; thus five sisters are still missing, allowing the four coffins sent to have contained the remains of four of them.

A gentleman who has seen the whole of the bodies has kindly given me the following account of their condition.

"M. H. Fontanier.—Head and face cloven to pieces with sword cuts. One spear wound through the chest.

M. Simon.—Head and face covered with sword cuts; body covered with numerous wounds; bowels protruding.

M. Thomasin.—Head and face covered with sword cuts; a few spear wounds on the body.

Madame Thomasin.—A sword cut through the back of the neck.

M. de Chalmaison.—Left side of the face cut away; eyes scooped out; numerous wounds in the body and extremities.

Madame de Chalmaison.—A deep sword cut across the face, just below the eyes; left arm and side hacked with sword cuts.

Father Chevrier.—Scull cloven in several places; chest and abdomen laid open; bowels protruding.

The coffins supposed to contain four of the Sisters were filled with charred pieces of flesh and bone.

Mr. Protopopoff, Russian.—Sword cut 5 inches long on the left side of the head; a spear wound through the chest, and one on the left hip.

Mrs. Protopopoff.—Body literally covered with sword cuts and spear wounds.

Mr. Basoff, Russian.—Head covered with sword cuts, chest pierced with numerous spear wounds.

Most of the bodies were in an advanced stage of decomposition, having been probably a good deal exposed to the sun on the banks of the river. They were all more or less naked, except Mr. Thomasin and wife.

It is reported that 180 children were brought to the yamên the day of the massacre; 30 children were found smothered in vaults,

supposed to be those either of the church or European hospital.
I consider that between 50 and 60 people must have perished in
the Sisters' places alone."

As a proof that the Chinese generally knew of the intended
attack, it may be mentioned that for several days previously
parents had been coming by day and night to take away their
children from the schools, so that out of about 450, only about
200 remained on the day of the fire. The 30 who were found
smothered must have run into the vault on the first alarm being
given. The shop-keepers about the Sisters' place also had for
some days been removing from their shops. The chefoo, or head
city magistrate, had posted a proclamation similar to those at
Chinkiang, and tending to excite the people against the foreigners. H. B. M.'s consul called the attention of Chung-How to
this proclamation on the 18th, three clear days before the outbreak, requesting him to pacify the people as the chefoo's proceedings were creating great disturbance in the city. On the
20th he again wrote to Chung-How, and for the third time, on
the morning of the 21st, the consul addressed an urgent despatch
to Chung-How, but received no reply to any of his communications.

I have noticed Chung-How's statement to the effect that he
accompanied M. Fontanier on his way back to the consulate.
At the meeting of the consuls he stated that M. Fontanier had
twice fired on him. Another mandarin told a foreign resident
here that he was one of two who were deputed by Chung-How
to accompany M. Fontanier to the consulate, that on the way
M. Fontanier said he did not want them, but 200 soldiers to drive
away the mob. A disturbance here arose close to the cathedral
and Fontanier and Simon were both killed. The story of Fontanier firing on Chung-How looks extremely like a fabrication of
the last named "excellent" gentleman.

There can be no doubt at all about the connivance of the authorities at this dreadful massacre, for even if it did not originate
with them, it was perfectly in their power to put down all display
of bad feeling when they were first requested to do so. They did
not choose to move a finger in this direction, but treated the
urgent appeals of the British consul with supercilious contempt.
No sooner, however, had the atrocious deed been perpetrated than
the authorities began to awake to a sense of what they had done,
and dread the consequences. This was first shewn when they

sent down the five coffins containing bodies, and with them three
empty coffins. The mandarin who brought them requested from
the British consul a receipt for the bodies, naming the consul's as
one of them. Again on the following day Chung-How sent a
special messenger to request a receipt for the six bodies, also mentioning the Consul's as being one of them, the request being of
course still refused. Once more the demand was made, and the
mandarin on this occasion received for answer that the body of
the consul which he professed to have brought, had actually been
picked up in the river on the previous evening; that it had been
recognised by several of deceased's friends, as well as identified by
the initials "H. F." on the socks. The mandarin feebly attempted to maintain that the consul's body was nevertheless one of the
five which he had brought, and for which he was ordered to
bring back a receipt to Chung-How. It must be remembered
that Chung-How had said the consul was killed by his side, and
that he had the body in his keeping. There was indeed one gentleman who was quite unable to recognise the body of poor M.
Fontanier, and he was a brother consul too. Perhaps he saw
with Chinese eyes, and believed against the evidence of his senses
that the murdered consul "might have been" in one of the coffins. Fortunately all foreigners who happen to be in Chinese
employ are not so easily converted to the Chinese mode of view-
ing things.

The Chinese authorities, cowardly as they are cruel, have be-
trayed abject fear of the consequences of what they have done, in
many ways since the dreadful occurrence took place. They have
requested the French minister at Peking to name his own terms
for compensation. They have asked the Russian friends of the
deceased here to name their conpensation, but were properly answered that they would know that from the Russian authorities.
At Taku they had couriers waiting, and two hours before the arrival of the *Opossum* gun-boat on the 26th, H. M.'s consul had a
letter requesting him not to allow the gun-boat to fire upon the
city. To-day again (27th) H. E. has asked the British consul to
apply for the acting appointment of French consul, when they two
could settle all matters between them. Altogether it seems as if
the native authorities had taken leave of their senses.

While deploring this melancholy occurrence I cannot help
thinking that it will result in good to China as well as to foreigners; and that the poor Sisters' death will bring forth more

fruit than they were permitted in their life time to see. The French nation cannot allow this deadly insult to pass unpunished —members of the embassy, of the consulate, and of the priest-hood—men and women—cruelly and treacherously murdered. Were they indeed to permit this crime to pass unpunished, no foreigner could with safety remain in China.

The Chinese are, naturally, endeavouring to conciliate the other Treaty-powers, it is to be hoped without effect; united they are as a bundle of sticks, strong, while individually they may easily be disposed of.

I understand 8 Protestant chapels in and about the city, are looted; 16 places of worship in all are said to have been destroyed. Many Catholic Christians are said to be murdered and thrown into the river; we have seen a good many bodies floating down with the tide. No Protestant converts have been killed, so far as is known, but they have been beaten and their houses pillaged, the Chinese afterwards offering to sell them the property they had stolen. There are any number of guilds here, banded to-gether for mischief, and the fire brigade are the parties who are said to have had the management of setting the buildings on fire, having the mob perfectly under control, calling them away when all was finished by the sound of the bell. More than one for-eigner heard this. The soldiers were present at the fires, and are said to have aided in the mischief, at least no one reports that they interfered in any way to prevent it. Now we hear that the city mob are turning against Chung-How, denouncing him as a friend to foreigners. His Excellency is evidently a weak-mided man, better suited for peace and war. He has been believed to be well-disposed to foreigners, though he has never shown it on any important occasion.

To-night a meeting has been held and a defence committee resolved upon, Mr. Hannen, Dr. Fraser and Mr. Hanna being members. The city is not yet quite quiet.

No. 3.

PLOCLAMATION BY CHUNG-HOW.

June 22nd, 1870.

A memorial has been presented to the throne by me, relating all the facts of the late strife stirred up by you people with the

French missionaries, and I am awaiting the imperial edict in answer. Whereas ever since Tientsin was opened as a port, all classes of natives and foreigners have always maintained friendship, it is incumbent on you to continue these peaceful relations with the foreigners who are living here. No disturbance can be permitted, and I have given orders to the civil and military authorities to apprehend and severely punish any persons who are found abusing or contending with foreigners in the streets or markets.

This proclamation is further issued to enjoin all classes to follow their peaceable callings. Arrest and execution will inevitably follow any attempt at a popular outbreak.

No consideration will be entertained. Let none disregard this special notice.

No. 4.

PROCLAMATION BY THE TIENTSIN CHE-HSIEN.

June 23rd, 1870.

The che-hsien has received the following despatch from the commissioner of trade (Chung-How):—

"I have already issued a notice on the subject of the massacre of missionaries and the burning of their churches, perpetrated by the mob on the 21st, in which the people were warned that immediate arrest and execution would overtake all who again attempted in their ignorance and stupidity to molest or loot any of the foreign hongs. We must now redouble our efforts to protect the consuls and all other foreigners in the various hongs in order to preserve amicable relations. I have therefore to direct the che-hsien to exercise his personal surveillance in protecting the foreign hongs, the customs, and the consulate in and about the Tze-Chu-Lin . Settlement.

If any malignant ruffians dare continue these disturbances, the che-hsien will immediately arrest and execute them without the least mercy, and he shall be answerable for any disturbances that may further take place through the laxity of his discipline."

Having received this despatch, the che-hsien sent out the police with orders to maintain an unflagging vigilance, and as in duty bound he issues this notice calling upon all classes to follow their proper duties. And they are hereby warned that if any foolish mob again attempts to molest a foreign hong, immediate arrest and execution will be incurred.

The che-hsien will not show the least relaxation in carrying out these instructions.

Beware of this special warning.

<hr>

No. 5.

IMPERIAL EDICT FROM THE GRAND SECRETARIAT.

June 25th, 1870.

A memorial has been received from Chung-How announcing that a quarrel had arisen between the people of Tientsin and the missionaries, resulting in a fight; for the occurrence of which he begged that he might receive his own punishment, and, at the same time, that the local authorities under him might be severally cashiered after a close enquiry into their conduct. This affair arose, on the one hand, through the Tientsin people suspiciously connecting the missionaries with the mysterious kidnapping of children which was being carried on by certain rogues—and their suspicions grew into hostility—on the other hand the French consul, Mons. Fontanier, enraged the populace by firing shots within Chung-How's yamên as well as at the che-hsien, and this brought on the emeute and his death, as also the burning and destruction of the churches.

Now, as Chung-How in his administration failed to preserve the public peace, and the Tientsin taotai Chow-Chih-Hsün, with whom lies the responsibility of enforcing general good behaviour, was yet unable to anticipate and prevent the disturbance, and the che-fu Chang-Kwang-Tsao, as well as the che-hsien, Liu-Chieh, managed so badly as to allow the matter to ferment into so serious an affair, all these officers have committed an error which they cannot throw off. Let the Li-pu accordingly consider their faults, and assign their punishment severally.   And Tsêng-Kwo-Fan is hereby ordered to proceed to Tientsin and hold an investigation on their conduct, whereon to rest the accusation. He will arrest the kidnappers and the ringleaders of the disturbance, and will also, in conjunction with Chung-How, institute a most searching and impartial enquiry and settle matters.

No. 6.

PROCLAMATION BY CHUNG-HOW.

June 25th, 1870.

Whereas on the 24th instant I received an Imperial Edict decreeing that Tsêng-Kwo-Fan was to come to Tientsin and act with me in investigating the occurrences connected with the destruction of the Roman Catholic mission, availing ourselves for the purpose of the general, the taotai and all the civil and military officers of the district, I hereby give notice that the Roman Catholic and Protestant missionaries have the Imperial sanction, expressed in the foreign Treaties, to their preaching their doctrines. And you should all know and recognise the fact. If any dare to molest the missionaries and fabricate stories to disturb the peace, they shall be rigorously apprehended and beheaded.

If you meet any foreigners in the street, either of the official or mercantile classes, or any native servants of theirs carrying letters, you will not be permitted to offer any hindrance whatever to their passage to and fro.   If you dare to disobey this wilfully, you will be very severely dealt with, and that without any extenuation.

A special notice.

No. 7.

It is asserted at Peking that some of the English speaking legations have already exculpated Chung-How from participation in the Tientsin massacre.   But we must refuse without further confirmation to give credence to such a rumour.   It would be premature to come to any conclusion on the subject until the case is thoroughly investigated; and none of the foreign ministers at Peking would be likely to be guilty of the indiscreton of pre-judging a grave question like the present in the absence of the proofs which the aggrieved parties may he prepared to bring for-ward. All the facts of the case, as far as they are yet known, tend with cumulative force to compromise the character of the local authorities, and further circumstantial evidence of their complicity will no doubt be forthcoming from day to day. It would be both illogical and unjust under such circumstances for any of the foreign representatives at Peking to accept the ready explanations which the Tsung-li yamên will doubtless offer them, and we should hardly think they would either be so impolitic or imprudent as to give an expression of opinion on the subject.

No. 8.

TIENTSIN.

(From our Correspondent.)

TIENTSIN, 30*th June,* 1870.

There are two Tientsin Protestant missionaries at present at stations in Shantung. One of them was heard from to-day, all well. With reference to the news of the attack here on the 21st, he mentioned that one of their preachers who had been within 170 *li* of Tsinanfoo on the 22nd, then and there heard that it was intended to attack foreigners on the 21st at Tientsin, and that there was to be a second attack on foreigners on the 24th. This shows how widely spread the rumour was, and how long a time before the event the attack was expected.

From the depositions of trustworthy Chinese, members of Pro-testant churches here, it would seem that the troubles began fully a month before the outbreak, about the beginning of the 5th month; when the interment of 30 to 40 bodies from the Catholic hospital took place. The coffins were new, but are believed to have contained nothing but bones. It was not even known whence they had come, or where they had died, some persons supposing they had died during winter, others that the bones

were those of bodies taken from some old burying-ground now
required for other purposes. The affair made a great noise, and
for a week or more hundreds visited the ground daily; the excitement constantly grew, and these interments, connected with
the rumours that children were being stolen and killed became
dangerous. Many of the coffins were opened and the bones
scattered, the grossest indignities and insults being heaped on
the remains of those who were supposed to have been Christians.

The kidnapping stories followed; two men being secured and
executed for the crime upon their own confession. Then came
the proclamation of the che-fu. The next rumour was that the
Sisters were in the habit of securing passers by, and this had such
an effect that the people dared not pass the hospital except in large
convoys! About this time (15th) the schools were closed in consequence of the story that foreigners intended to visit them for
the purpose of taking the scholars. About the 17th or 18th a
man was seized who said that he was commissioned by the
Catholics to kidnap, and that his chief was a native priest or
catechist at the cathedral, who supplied him with medicine and
gave him five dollars for expenses. In consequence of this statement the chefu visited the cathedral to look for the person
referred to, but although they were conducted all over the premises by foreigners, the kidnapper was unable to point out the
person he accused.

Nevertheless the mandarins paid repeated visits to the place,
and on the morning of the 23rd (Chinese moon) the che-fu went
again on the same errand. Large crowds had already assembled
on the banks of the river; a child threw a brick; this was resented by the servants of the consulate; the child followed and
the crowd took up the quarrel. The French officials went unarmed to Chung's yamên, whither the officials had already gone.
Chung sent with them several small officials to quiet the people,
but the disturbance broke out in one place as soon as it was
quelled in another. A rioter was at length seized, which made
matters worse. The officers were wounded and had to retreat.
The consul then sent for weapons and again went to Chung's
yamên. Report says the mandarin was twice fired at, a follower
of the che-hsien's being shot by the second ball. Chung then tried
to pacify the Frenchmen, and they gave up their weapons to his
officers. They were then conducted out of the yamên by these
men, Chung remaining in the yamên. The moment the foreigners

appeared in the street, the mob rose upon them. While they were at the yamên the riot had proceeded at the cathedral, and one Frenchman had been killed there, and the now enraged crowd fell upon the consul's party and killed them on their way back to the consulate, which was now given up to pillage, the gongs sounding the call all over the city.

The fire guild arriving at the bridge of boats were met by the che-hsien, who under orders from Chung endeavored to prevent the guilds south of the river from crossing, and the bridge began to be opened, just as either Chen-Chen-Tai or Chen-Tu-Suai (military officers) came up and wished to cross. According to Chinese custom this was at once permitted, and the guilds crossed with them, the officer shouting—"Haou hsiau, tsz! meng yung! Kwo chü! Kwo chü!" "Good young folks be brave and pass over." The guilds north of the river had however finished the work of slaughter, and nothing remained but to fire the buildings. Returning, the mob rushed off to the hospital, and began their task there.

Another account states that the scandals began about a month ago, and were to the effect that in the consulate and hospital children were killed and men employed to obtain them. On the Saturday forenoon I heard that the Catholic premises were to be burnt and the *foreigners* slain; heard this from many quarters. Heard the fire guilds called together by gongs, and having learned the intention of the people, knew for what purpose it was. Did not go to the consulate, but was present at the destruction of the hospital, standing near the back door. The premises were already in flames when I arrived, and the Sisters slain. The perpetrators were the fire guilds who when the deed was done were summoned to return by the usual call (hau-ling). Did not see the che-fu's proclamation; knew that the schools had been closed as the result of a rumour, but had no idea where it originated. This witness is of opinion that the literati would not have dared to do anything without a prior understanding with the magistrates, and that therefore, in any case, the latter are the guilty parties, especially the che-fu, to whom, he has reason to believe, testimonials were offered by the people three or four days before the outbreak, but were then declined by him with a "wait until it is all over."

Another witness states that he saw the first gong struck. It was a brass-basin, and the man who struck it *came out of Chung's yamên, after* the seizure and binding of a Frenchman in the yamên.

Another says that in the proclamation of the che-fu, issued after the two alleged kidnappers had been beheaded, neither the names or native places of the men were recorded; it is believed, in fact, that they were simple travellers and were slain without proper examination, or any evidence whatever that the children found with them were not their own. Subsequent to this proclamation, and in gratituede for it, the people in large numbers united in presenting an official umbrella and a tablet to the che-fu. These the witness saw in the Hu-pu-chie within the city. They were received by the magistrate, and the witness has been told that the bearers of them were presented with cakes, &c., by the magistrate. This was several days before the riot. Several literary men then began to prepare a paper for presentation to the che-fu, requesting to know where the two men who were beheaded came from, whose children they had stolen, and to whom they had sold the children for the purpose stated; also demanding why, without first punishing those who had been in the habit of buying the children, the officials had executed the men who were suspected of selling them; the gist of the whole being a complaint against the mandarins for having acted on mere suspicion.

Other witnesses give testimony similar to the above, and add that it was reported that Chen-Chen-Tai told the men to go forward and burn. At the destruction of the hospital one Chinese woman was taken from it and thrown into the river; but on promising to speak for the rioters and say she had been abducted, she was taken out. There are those here who saw all this. After the destruction of the hospital about 200 armed men resolved to march down on the Settlement with loud shouts, but were prevented by officers sent by Chung-How who told them their quarrel was with the French Catholics, and that other foreigners were not to be interfered with. This tallies exactly with the proclamation issued by Chung-How after the tumults had ceased.

It naturally occurs to one on hearing this, that if Chung-How had power to prevent an attack on the Settlement at the moment when the mob were excited by their cruel deeds, he could, with greater ease had he so wished, have prevented the attack on the French, the plan of which had been gradually maturing for a whole month before.

The second attack, which was intended to have taken place on Friday, is said to have been prevented by the che-hsien, who used all his power to do so.

July 1st.—An attack was again intended to have been made last night, according to native reports, a messenger having been sent to the settlement, about 10 P. M. to warn the missionaries. However, it is said to be postponed till the arrival of Tsêng-Kwo-Fan's armies when we are all to be annihilated. Rumour in Peking has it that Tsêng-Kwo-Fan has refused to go to Tien-tsin, giving no reason for so doing. Chung-How says that Tsêng is sick, and is allowed a week to rest himself. In the meantime he sends down two officers, a Tartar and a Chinese, to examine into affairs, but whether they were accompanied by troops or not, Chung-How did not know. Excitement among the people in Peking on Monday was increasing, but no immediate danger was apprehended. The Chinese ministers say there is nothing to fear; 2,000 troops were reported to be in the neighbourhood of the north cathedral as a guard. All the ministers in town have sent a note to Prince Kung declaring that this massacre will outrage the whole civilised world.

It is said that most people in the city here wish for Tsêng-Kwo-Fan's arrival, some thinking he will settle matters quietly, others that he will lead them on the foreigners and annihilate the latter at once! It is variously estimated that there are 8,000 to 10,000 men here who live by black-mail and plunder. These are the men who are creating, or rather carrying out the troubles according to order, and they have said they will rather fight Tsêng-Kwo-Fan than be taken by him. They threaten any foreigner who dares to cross to the east side of the river—that is where the Russians were killed. Chung-How is said to have but few troops here, and some of them not to be relied on. We are not aware of any of these rioters and murderers having yet been apprehended, and it is supposed that Chung is afraid to do so. I do not expect an attack on the Settlement, although it is by no means improbable that this would have been attempted, but for the presence of the two gunboats. On the arrival of the *Opossum* it was immediately reported in the city that she was short handed, and with equal alacrity the report spread on the arrival of the *Avon* that she had big guns on board.

Within the last few days the Chinese have desecrated the French cemetery situated close to the city. They have opened many of the graves, searching the coffins for treasure of one kind or another. To such lengths they will go!

Another body last night was sent down to the consulate by the Chinese authorities. The remains are reported charred, and to have on part of a chemise, and is therefore supposed to be a Sister's; they were buried this morning in the foreign cemetery at the Settlement beside the others.

It is reported from Peking that Chung-How goes home as ambassador to France to try and prevent war on account of this unfortunate affair. He is to be succeeded here by Ch'ung-Lin, of Corean extraction, but who has been long in Peking. He is highly spoken of as an intelligent young man. Two other changes are talked of, but the names are not given, neither is it stated who is to accompany Chung-How to France.

Mr. Peter Kirrulf, a Danish subject, and Mr. Benjamin of Messrs. E. D. Sassoon & Co.'s went to the city yesterday, but the Chinese merchants consider it is not advisable for foreigners yet to go there.

The *Dwarf* arrived this evening. By her we learn that you had received the news of the massacre. These arrivals will no doubt tend to tame the fierce spirit of the braves, who still go armed in the city and suburbs defying all to touch them.

I omitted to mention that I heard on good authority a few days ago that the che-fu, head city magistrate, was present at the burning of the cathedral, &c. He is said to be sorry for it now. He had no idea lives would be lost! An excuse for him that he had not been long here, and did not know the people. He is buying his experience at a heavy price.

The consuls have received a despatch from Chung-How to the effect that he has been appointed by the emperor to proceed to Paris.

No. 9.

TIENTSIN.

(From our Correspondent.)

4th July, 1870.

Since I last wrote all is evidently quiet. We have now a large fleet here, the *Avon, Dwarf, Opossum* and *Flamme* vessels of war, and the *Shanse, Nanzing, Shantung* and *Kiushu* merchant steamers. And this being the 4th of July, we have grand display of bunting from all of them.

The engrossing topic of conversation is of course the massacre. Chung-How is trying every means to exculpate himself; it is even reported that he has sent a circular letter to the native compradores stating that he was twice shot at by the French consul, and urging them to impress that fact on their employers. I hear the ministers at Peking exculpate him from blame. I hope he may be able to prove this.

The che-fu only arrived here about the end of April, and was at the time reported to have strong anti-foreign feelings. His name is Chang-Kwang-Swai. He and the che-hsien are on one side, and are opposed to Chung-How. The latter, it is said, wished to release the men who were falsely accused of kidnapping, but the che-fu took the responsibility on himself, saying he was not under the orders of Chung-How, but of Tsêng-Kwo-Fan, and he knew the execution of the two men would please the Vice-roy and the Emperor. He accordingly beheaded them, without having the legal power to do so, and without any form of trial. The bodies of the two men were afterwards cut in 10,000 pieces. Chung-How alone possesses the power of life or death here; in the tablet— Wang-ming-p'ai.

The name of the che-hsien is Liu-Chieh, who arrived here in 1868. He is a man of no education, a native of Yunan, and purchased his promotion. He professes to be more a foreigner than a Chinaman, but his professions are not highly esteemed. The name of the *Te-too* I have not heard mentioned; he is said to have been at one time a secretary to Chung-How, and is on his side. The general in command here is Chen-Ta-Shwai. It is he who led on the brave boys across the bridge of boats to attack and murder the defenceless Sisters of Mercy.

Cheng-Kwo-Jui is the general believed to have come from Tsêng-Kwo-Fan at Paoutingfoo, and who arrived here some days before the massacre. His professed errand to this place was to worship at the temple to San-Ko-Lin-Sin, who was his foster-father. He has since been in Peking and was received with honor by the Emperor, and is reported to have since returned to Tientsin.

Mr. Meadows goes home with Chung-How. They do not leave for a month. Mr. W. Jackson, formerly assistant to Mr. Meadows in his mercantile business, was lately appointed an assistant at the Imperial Arsenal, and is to take charge of it during Mr. Meadows' absence.

The French have erected at the British consulate a flag-staff, on which to hoist the French flag. The 15 policemen sent up by the *Shantung,* return by the *Shanse,* much disappointed not to have seen some service in the north. A number of native braves have gone to Taku; disturbances are expected there, and *Opossum* goes to watch.

The scurrilous letter from Tientsin in the *Daily News* of June 28th is not likely to pass unanswered. * * * was at Tsinanfoo on the 28th and wrote to his partner here on that day. He had evidently not heard the report, but he remarks on the strange looks all the people gave him, which he could not account for. This shows that the news of the doings at Tientsin had reached Tsinanfoo, but at what date was uncertain.

Another letter says:—You know I am not an alarmist, but I do now most deliberately say that things are about as gloomy as they can be. Our natives are much alarmed, and speak of the demonstrations in the city, and specially in the suburbs east of the river as most menacing. They have just come in with the report that Tsêng-Kwo-Fan's troops are encamped within ten or fifteen *li* of Tientsin, and that the leaders in these hostilities against foreigners are openly calling on the people to volunteer for service in an organised attack. They are exultant at the arrival of Tsêng-Kwo-Fan's men, and say that victory is now most certainly on their side. These statements may indicate little more than foolish bravado, but they at any rate prove that, even though there may not be the ability, there is certainly the will to utterly extinguish the foreign element.

No. 10.

PEKING.

The following interesting particulars are from a letter dated Peking, July 2nd.

The rumour referred to as current in Peking, however absurd in themselves, are important as showing the way the wind blows. The idea that runs through them all is of foreigners to be got rid of, by craft and force; and the careful way in which the French are singled out, even in these popular rumours, as the object of present aversion, well illustrates the *divide et impera* principle on which, it is understood, the Chinese government has been ably prompted by some of its advisers, as the best means of controlling the barbarians. How fatally successful they have already been in playing off one foreign representative against another is only too palpable.

"I don't wonder at your incredulity when I tell you that the apathy of the English-speaking legations is greater than ever. The U. S. have proposed to the Chinese to send a member of the Tsung-li yamên to Paris to manage this, in accordance with the usage of civilized nations, but the Chinese are better than their teachers. On Wednesday 22nd they addressed an identical note to the foreign legations that Chung-How would go to Paris, and Chung-Lin (member of the Foreign Board, hated by some at least of his foreign acqaintances here) would take Chung-How's place at Tientsin. Rochechouart lets them go on following their blind foolish guide, but that the French mean real hard hitting, is doubted by those only who are so busy conning their own theories of causes, &c., and their own despatches, that they don't go near the French. Chung-How will probably go, he having been proposed for France two years ago, and being able to pay his own way, * * * may go with him, or perhaps a greater white man still. Money works wonders.

More important, I fear, is the report here that Chen-Kwo-Jui, the old Mahomedan Taiping, who alone broke down the che-hsien and led the braves across the bridge, has arrived here, had an audience of the Emperor, and has returned to Tientsin in high favor. This man, I learn, came up from Yangchow, reaching Tientsin only 3 or 4 days before Tuesday, and it seems to be only along his route to the north that these astounding proclamations against the Frenchmen, printed *before* Tuesday, were found. These proclamations * * * will not listen to; he says until he sees will not believe in them, and his tone indicates *not even then.......* I believe that those proclamations are the prints which track Chen-Kwo-Jui from his mischief making at Nankin to the outbreak waiting his first arrival at Tientsin, if indeed his second arrival in Tientsin to-day from the reception of a pleased sovereign, do not prove the signal of a fresh outbreak. Whether Tsêng-Kwo-Fan be merely a blind old man and a tool, time will show.

Stories go here that the nuns were ravished, natives boiled to broth, 2,500 French killed, that the English and Americans indignant at French sorcery will fight the French, even should the

Chinese hold their hand. They only see * * * remember, who hates * * * * as he does the devil. They also speak of Taku manned, of the Yangtsze closed by Chinese gun-boats, &c. Rumours without number.

The Emperor's first edict was the Friday after the massacre, to the effect that a "foreign consul" had penetrated the yamên, fired at the che-hsien, and been killed by the outraged populace, who had burnt the cathedral; no other murders mentioned. "Let Tsêng-Kwo-Fan and Chung-How examine and find who is guilty." Verdict of every reader upon such a statement, "foreigner guilty."

Excitement consequently grew fast, as upon the che-fu's proclamation in Tientsin. Notice of the yamên was immediately called to this offensive edict, but not till Tuesday came out edict No. 2, saying nothing of foreign fire-arms, laying blame on whoever implicated foreigners in bad practices, and threatening with death whosoever should get foreigners into trouble again by implicating them with kidnappers anywhere in the empire. Tsêng alone to examine. The officials to be brought to the Li-pu and degraded. Wednesday 22nd Chung-How appointed to Paris as above.

Monday 27th excitement was highest. Children taken from school in fright; one boy forcibly carried off at Tungchow in fright; several teachers ran away, and another two days would have sent our servants packing. Rumours that the English legation was *sealed up* by the officials, &c. Stones flung at one foreign lady; another detained by a crowd in front of the cathedral refused passage, except on payment of cash, followed and hooted. We came very near repeating the Tientsin programme.

The edict No. 2 soothed the mob down in 24 hours, and everything is quiet since.

It is a fact that the Sisters allowed men from the crowd the week before the massacre, to enter and examine for themselves; that Fontanier rebuked the Sisters for it, expelled the che-hsien, and I believe the che-fu, on Monday when they called at the consulate and demanded an official examination. Report goes that "the legations all exculpate Chung-How." The French, I am inclined to believe, care little what the others think. They smoke and look unconcerned, mischief is brewing I am confident, notwithstanding that every official opinion discountenances this. I believe that if the Chinese find they have missed the fighting man, not only at Yangchow in the English, but also at Tientsin in the

French, they will try the English and Americans again, and next time make it wholesale.

Some 6,000 troops have returned from the camp a few miles out of the city, and are now in their homes here, subject to the call of the moment. The *country* is quite safe as far as I have seen. Feeling is made to order here very fast. Forty-eight hours would render the city unsafe at any time that a few powerful mandarins agreed, and the extinguisher is put on, with like abruptness when they please.

No. 11.

TIENTSIN.

By the *Manchu* we have the unexpected news that Chung-How has been ordered to Paris. The object of thus shifting the venue is of course plain enough. Encouraged by the success of the Burlingame Mission in hoodwinking the European governments, the Peking authorities probably believe that everything disagreeable may be avoided by simply "explaining matters" to the French Emperor, and begging him to consider the "difficulties" of China. But on this occasion the impudence of the Peking government has probably over-reached itself. The idea of sending the man who is charged with the blackest outrage on the French nation and on humanity that has ever been committed in China, as *Ambassador* to the power that has been so insulted, shows how little the mandarins have yet learned of international decency. The Emperor of China will not condescend to receive the *minister* of France, but. the Emperor of the French is expected to receive one whom we must regard as at least *responsible for the murder* of French subjects! Chung-How is to be succeeded by one Chung-Lin.

The British consul asked Chung-How if it was safe for foreigners to return to the city. H. E. advised a little more delay, and notified the same to British and French subjects. On the 29th Mr. J. A. T. Meadows went up to the city, and on his return issued a circular stating where he had been, that he was in plain clothes and unattended, that he met with no molestation, and that he considered it quite safe for foreigners to go there. I understand he went in his capacity of American consul to look after American interests. This morning (30th June) the Protestant missionaries—

4

alas, there are no others now—desirous of going to see their flocks, consulted their converts as to the advisability of visiting the city, mentioning that Mr. Meadows had gone up yesterday. The converts smiled, and said that placards were posted all over the town saying that Mr. Meadows was coming to the city, and advising everyone to be quiet and peaceable towards him. The converts also reported that Mr. Meadows had a guard of several men at no great distance who never lost sight of him, in case of any attack; and that they did not consider it safe for a foreigner to go to the city at present; that though the large majority of the people were well-inclined towards foreigners, yet there were many bad men in various parts of the city who are not to be trusted; they therefore strongly advised the missionaries not to venture at present in the city. Before Mr. Meadows went up, it was generally reported that he was to have ten mandarins to accompany him.

The *Dwarf* arrived on 1st July.

No. 12.

As a further contribution to the history of the Tientsin massacre, we give the following statements made by a Chinese who is considered a trustworthy man:—

Before a riot he heard from a hsin-tai that there had been a meeting of some literary men at the yamên connected with the Wen-hseo, the temple of Confucius, when a paper was prepared having reference to the *yau yen* and presented to the mandarins. This was besides a matter of common report. The witness believes this affords a clue to the origin of the troubles, because,

1st.—The meeting in question preceded the issue of the obnoxious proclamation by the fu.

2nd.—The closing of the native schools followed at once.

3rd.—All the fire-guilds have literary men at their head.

4th.—The *i-mien* volunteer forces which were originated at the time of the Tai-ping rebellion, are also headed by men who hold literary degrees, a list of these, as of the leaders of the fire-guilds, being kept in the hsien's yamên. These *i-mien* are legally privileged to bear arms; and they formed the armed portion of the crowd on Tuesday the 21st June; they assembled at the signal used by the fire-guilds, proving a preconcerted arrangement between them; such an agreement was necessarily made by the leaders, who again can hardly be supposed to have gone so far without the approval of the literati and local authorities.

The literati who waited upon the Lau-sz were five in number, their names were not known to witness.

In Tientsin there is a Shensz', now or formerly the hsin-tai of Taku, a red button, very wealthy, influential and a Mahomedan. This man was seen to be specially active in the attack on the French Consulate. The murder of Monsieur Chalmaison and his wife, and the plunder of their house was the work of Mahomedans alone.

The Mahomedans are now in the constant habit of meeting outside the west gate and elsewhere, and a Mahomedan rising is seriously feared by many.

The Chean-hang, Cho-hang, Ten-hang, &c., indeed almost all the corporations by which money is squeezed out of the people have Mahomedans at their head, and it sometimes happens that a Buddhist or other religionist is got rid of by foul means to make room for a Mahomedan in such posts.

Our correspondent, who has taken pains to inform himself accurately of the practice of the Sisters of Mercy in regard to receiving children, writes:

I have conversed with three gentlemen who had visited the Sisters' establishment only a few days before the massacre. One of them says that when speaking of the Chinese reports a Sister informed him they never paid a cash for a child, and that they could fill their place twice over with children that were offered to them.

A second quotes another Sister who told him that parents had frequently brought their children declaring that, if the Sisters would not receive them, it would be necessary to drown them, as the parents were too poor to support them. The Sisters had often taken in children under such circumstances even when they had properly no room for them. The parents of the children had always access to them. The Sisters had occasionally given a few cash to support the parents when they were very poor.

The third gentleman, whose duty frequently called him to the Sisters' establishment, states that he has seen the children at play, neat and clean, and apparently as happy and contented as children generally are, and he has also frequently seen as many as 40 or 50 women there on Sunday, the mothers of the children who had come to visit them. Many of the children were blind.

Writing on July 7th.   Our correspondent says:

Several gentlement and a lady arrived here yesterday from Peking by boat.   They were repeatedly asked by the way whether they were English, after which they passed safely on.   They report that the French consulate seemed completely razed to the ground.   The walls and tower of the cathedral are standing, as is also the *Cross* at the apex of the roof.

No. 13.

CHEFOO.

The following is an authentic account of the *Marchu's* stay at Chefoo.

Arrived at Chefoo 3rd July, at 2.10 p.m.; at 9 p.m. great excitement amongst the foreign community, in consequence of rumours that the foreigners are to be attacked to-night.   Loaded the guns on board of the steamer and took all the ladies and children on board.

At a meeting held to-day, 4th July, at Messrs. Wilson, Cornabé & Co.'s, Mr. Mayers, the British consul, in the chair, it was voted that the *Manchu* be requested to remain at Chefoo until the next steamer arrived.

Our correspondent writes:—"The community of Chefoo feel deeply grateful to Capt. Steele of the *Manchu* for detaining his steamer to render assistance in case of need."

When the *Manchu* left Chefoo, at 7 p.m. on the 5th July, all was again quiet.   The panic seems to have been caused by the disappearance of many of the Chinese servants from the foreign hongs, which was thought to betoken some attack.   But well informed people seem to think that the disappearance of the servants was caused by a dread among them of foreign vengeance.   The arrival of a number of junks from Tientsin, the crew of which had gone ashore, was probably the cause of the panic among the domestics.   It is said that when the alarm arose, and foreigners began to look to their weapons, not more than 12 effective rifles or muskets could be found.   A requisition came down per *Manchu* for a supply of Sniders.

No. 14.

PEKING.

SINISTER rumours were current in the capital immediately after the massacre of Tientsin, but we learn that the appearance of the imperial edict in the Gazette on the 27th, ordering an investigation into the Tientsin business had a great effect in allaying public anxiety. The copious rain that had fallen is also supposed to have had a great effect on the native mind.

There appears to be a deep-rooted superstition among the Pekingese that the spires of Pe-tang (Catholic church) being higher than the imperial palace and all the temples, draws away the luck from the Chinese to foreigners, and is a great cause of drought and famine. This idea is said to have gained a certain currency in the neighbouring provinces. The populace of Peking, though free from any ill-feeling against foreigners, might easily be excited to commit atrocities by a judicious use being made of these superstitions by the authorities.

No. 15.

The following address of sympathy has been sent to-day to the Reverend fathers of the Society of Jesus, of the Order of Lazarus, and of the Board of Foreign Missions in Shanghai, by the Protestant Clergy and missionaries residing in the settlement:—

We, the undersigned Protestant Clergymen and missionaries residing at Shanghai, lose no time in writing to assure you of our profound and sincere sympathy on the present occasion. At a time like this one unanimous feeling of common sorrow fills our hearts. The loss of the devoted men and women, who have been so barbarously sacrificed at Tientsin, is a loss to all Christendom. Deep and terrible, however, as is the calamity, we cling to the promise of Our Lord Jesus Christ, that He will be with His people to the end of the World, and we are comforted by the teaching of Ecclesiastical History, which assures us, that 'the blood of Martyrs is the Seed of the Church.' We pray that full reparation for the past,

and better protection for the future may be secured for those engaged in the spread of Religion throughout the Chinese empire.
   Shanghai, July 5th, 1870.

       (Signed),

           THOS. MCCLATCHIE,
                M. A. Canon of St. John's Cathedral, Hongkong,
                and Missionarh of the Ch. Miss. Society.

           CHARLES HENRY BUTCHER,
                M. A. Canon of St. John's Cathedral, Hongkong.
                British Consular Chaplain, Shanghai.

           WILLIAM MUIRHEAD,
           GEO. S. OWEN,
           JAMES THOMAS,
                 Members of the London Mission.

           J. W. LAMBUTH,
           YOUNG J. ALLEN,
                 Members of the Wesleyan Epis. Church Miss.,
                 U. S. A.

           J. M. W. FARNHAM,
                 Am. Presby. Mission.

           KARL KREYER,
           ROBERT NELSON,
                 Presbyter Am. Pryst. Epis. Mission, Snanghai.

           E. W. SYLE,
                 Seamen's Chaplain.

           JOHN WHERRY,
                 Am. Presbyter. Mission, Shanghai.

   The following reply has been addressed by the French missionaries, to the letter condolence which we publish yesterday.

   À Messieurs les Membres du Clergé Protestant et Missionnaires,
resident à Shanghaï.

   MESSIEURS,—En réponse à la lettre collective que vous avez
bien voulu nous adresser hier, nous avons l'honneur de vous dire
combien nous avons été touchés de cette marque de sympathie, et
combien nous avons apprecié les nobles sentiments qui l'ont dictées.

   Cette marque de sympathie de nous a été d'autant plus agréable
que nous avions été péniblement affectés par certaines correspon-
livrées au public, et dont le caractère n'est pas moins regrettable
par la fausseté des récits que par la malveillance des insinuations
qu'elles contiennent.

Nous aurions pu, sur le champ rétablir la vérité des faits dénaturés, et justifier l'innocence calomniée ; mais confiants dans le bon sens public, et assurés que la vérité saura se faire jour, quand même, nous avons préféré garder le silence.

Quelle que soit l'amertume de notre douleur, ce n'est pas pour nous une faible consolation de penser que Dieu, qui sait toujours tirer le bien du mal, fera tourner à sa plus grande gloire les lamentables évènements qui attristent en ce moment tous les cœurs honnêtes.

Nul doute que le sang de tant d'innocentes victimes si inhumainement répandu, s'élevant de l'autel de l'agneau, ne crie pour nous et n'obtienne la seule vengeance que nous ambitionnons : une plus grande diffusion de la vraie lumière sur ce peuple assis à l'ombre de la mort, et un plus libre exercice des œuvres de charité à l'égard de tous les malheureux, et surtout de l'enfance qui fut pour notre divin Sauveur l'objet d'une prédilection si marquée.

Shanghaï, 6 Juillet, 1870.

A. AYMERI,
Prêtre Lazariste.

H. BASUIAU,
S. J.

E. LEMONNIER,
Mis. Ap. Procureur des Missions Etrangères.

[*Translation.*]

To the Clergymen and members of the Protestant missions, residing at Shanghai.

GENTLEMEN,—In reply to the letter which you have had the goodness to address to us jointly, yesterday, we have the honour to inform you how much we have been moved by the token of your sympathy, and how greatly also we have appreciated the high sentiments on your part that prompted it. Your mark of sympathy has been a double pleasure to us, since we had been painfully grieved by some correspondence published in the papers, the character of which is not less to be deplored for the falseness of the recital, than for the ill-will displayed, and for the insinuations contained. We might have immediately re-established the truth against perversion, and justified innocence over calumny ; but trusting to the sound common sense of the public, and feeling sure that truth must come out under any circumstances, we had preferred keeping silence. However bitter is our sorrow, yet it is no small consolation for us when we reflect that God, who ever knows how to bring good out of evil, knows also how to change for His greatest glory, these present lamentable occurrences, so saddening to very upright heart. No doubt the blood of so many innocent victims, so barbarously shed, must rise up to the Altar of the Lamb, and cry loud on our behalf, till it obtains for us the sole vengeance we wish for, viz. the better spread of the true light on these people now living under the shadow of death; the greater freedom for the better exercise of works of charity towards the suffering, and principally towards the little ones who were, for our Divine Saviour, objects of such singular affection.

(Signed) A. AYMERI,
               Prêtre Lazariste.

          H. BASUIAU,
               S. J.

          E. LEMONNIER,
               Procurator of Mission Etrangère.

No. 16.

ADDRESS TO THE MISSIONARIES OF THE ROMAN CATHOLIC MISSION AT NINGPO.

REVEREND SIRS,—We the undersigned Protestant missionaries at this port, beg to tender to you an expression of our sincere sympathy, on the occasion of the barbarous murder of so many of your fellow-countrymen and fellow-laborers at Tientsin.

Whatever difference of opinion as to religious matters may unhappily divide us, we cannot allow it to suppress the natural feeling of deep sorrow which arises in all our hearts, for the terrible loss you have sustained; nor the profound sense of indignation we entertain towards the perpetrators of a deed, which is an outrage alike against the spirit of Christianity, and our common humanity.

Our earnest prayer, however, in the face of this most distressing event, is that the great Disposer of all things may overrule it to the increased security of European life, and the increased extension of our Redeemer's Kingdom in this unhappy country.

Trusting that you will kindly accept this expression of our most cordial sympathy with you under your very deep trial,

We beg to subscribe ourselves,

Reverend Sirs,

Yours most respectfully,

(Signed,)   1.—THOMAS H. HUDSON,
    English General Baptist Mission.

2.—E. C. LORD,
    American Baptist Mission.

3.—W. A. RUSSELL,
    Church of England Mission.

4.—CONRAD BASCHLIN,
    English & Continental Baptist Mission.

5.—JAMES BATES,
    Church of England Mission.

6.—ROBERT PALMER,
    Church of England Mission.

7.—J. A. LEYENBERGER,
    American Presbyterian Mission.

8.—JOHN BUTLER,
    American Peesbyterian Mission.

9.—FREDERICK GALPIN,
    Methodist Free Church Mission.

10.—J. R. GODDARD,
    American Baptist Mission.

11.—H. JENKINS,
    American Baptist Mission.

12.—D. L. LYON,
    American Presbyterian Mission.

13.—J. BARCHET,
    Baptist Missionary.

Ningpo, 8th July, 1870.

[*Translation.*]

SIRS,—It was not without very deep emotion that I read yesterday evening, the address of sympathy which you have condescended to address to us on the occasion of the massacre at Tientsin.

If we looked at this event only with the cold indifference of reason, we might well despair of a nation which violates so openly the rights of men.

But, as disciples of Jesus Christ, we know that it was by the cross that he saved the world, and his well-beloved disciple adds that "if He died for us, we ought also to die for our brethren." Moreover, there is history to prove that the blood of Christians is ever a fruitful seed which multiplies itself a hundredfold.

Let us then hope that God, without whose will not a hair of our head falls, has permitted this sad catastrophe only for the salvation of the Chinese nation, and that He will get glory from it.

Begging you to accept my sincere thanks and those of all my brethren, whose spokesman I am,

I have the honor to be, Sirs,

Your very humble servant,

I. MONTAGNEUX,
Pr. Vic. of Chekiang.

Ningpo, 9th July, 1870.

No. 17.

ADDRESS OF THE GERMAN COMMUNITY OF TIENTSIN TO COUNT ROCHECHOUART.

[*Translation.*]

TIENTSIN, 21st July, 1870.

To Count Rochechouart,
H. I. M.'s Chargé d'Affaires in China.

M. le Comte,

In view of the events of the 21st June, which have torn away so many unhappy victims from among your countrymen, the

German residents of Tientsin, being now enabled by your arrival from Peking to express their feelings to the chief representative of the French nation in China, are animated by a unanimous desire to express to you their most profound and cordial sympathy.

We feel the more prompted to do this, as the faithfulness shown by your consul and missionaries, in the fulfilment of their several duties has filled us with the most sincere respect, and as we have always revered the beneficent activity and the zeal regardless of danger of the Sisters of Charity. At the same time we are fully aware of the community of interests which all foreigners have in these sad occurrences.

The undersigned beg of you, M. le Comte, kindly to bring this expression of our sympathy to the knowledge of your countrymen.

(Nine Signatures.)

———————

[*Translation.*]

TIENTSIN, 22nd July, 1870.

To P. Wentzel, Esq.,
 Consul of the North-German Confederation of Tientsin.

  Monsieur le Consul,

I have received the letter which you did me the honour to write me yesterday, together with the address which the German community of Tientsin have sent me with reference to the events of the 21st June and the massacre, so sad for us, of 17 innocent French subjects.

It is certainly a great consolation, after such a cruel disaster, to feel one's self surrounded by so much sympathy. I hasten therefore, Monsieur le Consul, to tell you how deeply I have been affected by this act of your countrymen, which I shall not fail to bring to the knowledge of my government. And I beg of you to act as my interpreter with them, in thanking them, both for their interest in our grief, and for their flattering praises of the victims of this abominable outrage, which will, I hope, be punished in the way it deserves.

I avail myself of this opportunity to assure you, etc.

(Signed)   ROCHECHOUART.

No. 18.

THE FUNERAL SERVICE.

The funeral service for the victims of the Tientsin massacre was held on the morning of the 8th July at 9 o'clock in the French church. The building was hung with black and a large catafalque draped with crape erected in the centre aisle. The regular church service was performed:—High mass for the dead with the absolution. It began with *"Dies iræ, dies illa;"* after mass, a procession was formed round the catafalque, after which were sung as is customary *Libera nos Domine de morte æterna;* and the *Kyrie Eleison.* On the black hanging in front of the organ gallery was the moto HODIE MIHI CRAS TIBI. The only specialities were the catafalque and black drapery.

The priest who said mass was Father Della Corte, Superior General of the mission of Kiangnan.

A body of sailors from the French men-of-war now in harbour were drawn up in the centre aisle, and were supported by a detachment of armed police. The attendance was very numerous, and indicated unmistakeably the deep sympathy which the event has called forth in men of all creeds and nationalities. We noticed nearly all the consuls for the various European nations and the acting consul for the United States, the assistant Judge of the Supreme Court and other officials. The Municipal Council attended in a body, and several of the resident Protestant Clergy, testified their respect for the feelings of their Roman Catholic brethren by being present. The flags of the ships in harbour and of the various consulates were half-mast high.

No. 19.

THE "PAPER-MAN" AT CHINKIANG.

SHANGHAI, 9th July, 1870.

To the Editor of the
   "SHANGHAI EVENING COURIER."

SIR,—For some days past, the Chinese at Chinkiang and Yangchow have been considerably excited over a most absurd rumour. The story seems to be gaining credence amongst the

Chinese very fast, and as it illustrates their blind credulity—to say the least—I beg permission to give the readers of the *Courier* a brief account of the rumour, as it was given to me by a gentleman who resides in Chinkiang.

It is supposed that the "paper man," (that is the name by which the rumour is known) is a kidnapper. He is spoken of as a "foreigner" by the Chinese, and his reputed object is to kidnap, kill, or injure the natives; and in order to accomplish his object without the possibility of detection, he *transforms himself*, by the aid of some mysterious power, *into paper!* At times, it is asserted, he will appear as a scrap of plain paper; at other times he comes in the guise of an old newspaper. A favorite dodge with him is to *get himself made into a kite.*

He thereby accomplishes his object, of getting into people's houses with greater facility.

At all events, he contrives, while "out of the flesh," to have *wind blow him into the houses*, or gets carried in by some means; there he lies as a piece of paper until all the inmates go to bed at night. When all the family are asleep, suspecting no danger, doors are fastened, the "paper man" assumes the flesh again and carries out his diabolical designs.

As soon as it was reported that the "paper man" had come, the people sought the advice of some wise man, and he advised that a basin of water, *which had been used for bathing by the female members of the various families, be kept in each house, and that every piece and scrap of paper be sprinkled with that water.* One drop of it, would certainly give the "paper man" his quietus. Of course the foolish people are all hunting up bathing water, and sprinkling all the old scraps of paper, and they seem to have great faith in the remedy. Ridiculously absurd as the story is, there can be no doubt that the mass of the people believe it. Short notices are posted thickly through the city at Chinkiang, and also at Yangchow, notifying all to beware! the "paper man" is coming! Look out for the "paper man!" &c. &c.

I only speak of the rumour, Mr. Editor, as an instance of Chinese credulity and gullibility. Should any one regard it in the light of a joke, let him reflect that the same stupid ignorance that engenders and fosters such absurdities, has already given us all just cause for deepest sorrow.—Yours truly,

CREDULUS.

No. 20.

There was a certain degree of panic and disturbance in the French Concession on the night of the 12th, but rumour, as is customary, has greatly exaggerated the reality. We have heard it positively asserted that the Fathers at Tunkadoo had received such threatenings that they thought it prudent to seek the protection of the Settlement; that 60 men were landed from the *Zebra* and patrolled the Bund till midnight; that all the ladies on the French side had left it, &c. &c. This is very wide of the truth. It is true that two priests came in from Sicawei yesterday to make certain enquiries, but they reported all tranquil and friendly around them. Indeed special agents have been employed by the authorities to ascertain whether proclamations were, as has been alleged, being posted in the surrounding neighbourhood. And their united report is that within a radius of 8 miles not one such proclamation has been seen. But a rumour that the Tunkadoo cathedral, the French church, and the French Concession generally, were to be attacked last night, assumed such proportions shortly after 8 p. m. that the French police and volunteers were ordered out. The French consul-general saw them properly posted and gave orders that no Chinese were to be allowed to enter the Concession from the city, and that they were to use their weapons only if attacked. Consul Medhurst and Capt. Denison of the *Zebra* were ready to render assistance if necessary. Some mandarin, said by some people to have been the taotai, though that is very unlikely, came with a large number (about 200) soldiers down to the bridge which separates the Concession from the riverside suburb, and wished to come down to render assistance. But the piquet stationed there refused to let them pass, in terms of Count Mejan's orders, and they were forced to retire, the mandarin expressing his wrath in a loud and violent manner. The piquet was several times assailed with stones by the crowds behind the barrier across the bridge; but when a warning was given the assailants that if they threw any more, they would be fired on, they at once desisted. The patrols were not withdrawn till about 3 a. m. Through some mistake a party of men was landed from the *Zebra* and posted round the British consulate, but they were sent on board immediately on Mr. Medhurst's return from the French side. Altogether, this slight disturbance may be productive of good, it must have shown the natives that we are on the alert. Two days ago the taotai informed Count Mejan that the Franco-Chinese battalion (300 men) near the South gate were at his disposal, under the command of M. Pallu de la Barrière, and Count Mejan has requested that they be employed to guard Tunkadoo and Sicawei. It appears also that proclamations which the Viceroy Ma agreed to publish in terms of Count Rochechouart's demand when he visited Nankin have up to this time remained unpublished. But as the result of a severe letter of Count Mejan to Ma, some hundred copies of the proclamation have been sent to the taotai to be posted up throughout his district.

No. 21.

PROCLAMATION BY MA, VICE-ROY OF THE TWO KEANG; AND TING, GOVERNOR OF KEANGSU.

May 24th, 1870.

It is stated in the 13th Art. of the French Treaty that "the Christian religion having for its object the exhortation of men to do good, its converts shall enjoy the fullest protection to their persons and property, and shall be free to meet together for the performance of the worship and chants of their religion. The local authorities must treat the missionaries with respect, and afford them protection. No interference shall be offered to such as wish to embrace the religion and practise its rites. All former notices whatsoever prohibiting the doctrine of Christianity, no matter where they were promulgated, must be annulled and removed."

The 6th Article of the supplementary Treaty states, that "French missionaries can follow their own will in buying land or building houses in any province."

Now these converts, for all they embrace a new doctrine are yet Chinese subjects, and their teachers inculcate respect and obedience to the Sovereign, and a careful observance of the laws and statutes of China. Of course, then, they must be treated with the same kindness (as you show to Chinese), and so exemplify the wish to regard all with equal benevolence.

The Tsung-li yamên obtained an Imperial Edict directing the Vice-roys and governors to compel the local authorities to deal promptly and equitably with all matters affecting the converts;

and not to allow them either to attach such importance as suited themselves to the cases, or intentionally to delay their settlement, and thereby oppress the converts. All this is on record; and the above orders must of course be followed out. Yet, of late, in several places, people have opposed their procuring land or erecting churches, and have created disturbances relying on their numbers.

Although the local authorities received strict orders from the Vice-roys and governors, to apprehend and punish the rioters, yet they have been unable in some cases to put a speedy end to the disturbances.

The French minister, M. Rochechouart, treated the matter in accordance with the treaty.

Hereafter the people and missionaries, wherever they happen to be collocated, must preserve a lasting friendship and respect for each other. It will not do to stir up any more commotions.

It is right that we should issue a clear proclamation on this point. And this proclamation is hereby issued, for the information of all within our jurisdiction, both soldiers and civilians. You are to know that the Treaty sanctions both the preaching and the embracing of these doctrines, while those who don't care to be converted cannot be compelled to do so. You are not, therefore, to offer perverse opposition.

These missionaries have come from abroad, with the set purpose of inculcating virtue; and it is all the more necessary therefore to treat them with courtesy.

After the issue of this proclamation, everyone must observe the Treaty; it will not do to make an appearance of complying while you secretly break it. The law will be applied with extra severity if there is any more rioting, and clemency will be impossible.

A necessary proclamation.

No. 22.

PROCLAMATION BY THE TAOTAI OF SHANGHAI.

Tu, the taotai of the circuit of Soochow, Sungkiang and Tai-tsing makes a proclamation.

Whereas it is laid down in the 18th Article of the British Treaty that the Chinese authorities shall at all times afford the fullest protection to the persons and property of British subjects, whenever these shall have been subjected to insult or violence, and in such case shall "at once arrest guilty parties, whom they will punish according to law;" And

Whereas the 36th Article of the French Treaty provides that "if any French subject shall sustain any injury, or if they are insulted or outraged by any Chinese subjects, the offenders shall be sought for by the local authorities, who will take all necessary steps for the protection of the French"—"and having arrested the guilty parties punish them with the utmost force of the law;" Moreover

Whereas the 11th Article of the American Treaty states that "all citizens of the United States of America in China, peaceably attending to their affairs, shall have their persons and property fully protected from insult or injury, by the local authorities, and that any Chinese guilty of violence towards United States citizens shall be punished by the Chinese authorities according to the laws of China.

Now, at the port of Shanghai trade is carried on between Chinese and foreigners, and up to the present they have lived together in amity as one family; whilst the local authorities, in accordance with the Treaties have protected the persons and property [of all foreigners]; but lately some utterly lawless persons, whose names are unknown, have posted up inflammatory placards against foreigners, evidently with the intention of fomenting discord. The taotai's hatred is roused against [these offenders], and he has ordered the local authorities, and all officials here most carefully to search for and to arrest these criminals and punish them most severely.

The taotai now issues this proclamation, and commands every Chinaman, peaceably and in accordance with law, to look after his own special business and not to attend to these placards or be afraid of foreigners. If hereafter any persons shall post up inflammatory placards against foreigners, they shall be arrested and punished with the utmost rigour of the law;—they will have no chance of escaping from this.

Let all men most respectfully attend to this proclamation.

Tung Chih 9th year, 6th moon, and 16th day (July 14th, 1870).

      True Translation
      Harry Parkes McClatchie.

No. 23.

TIENTSIN.

July 11*th*, 1870.

Tsêng-Kwo-Fan arrived here a few days since. An eye witness (Chinese) reports that on the 9th several mandarins of high rank —red buttons—went to the cemetery in which the Sisters of Mercy buried their dead from the hospital, and had several coffins dug up. Bodies, or skeletons, were found with eyeless sockets which some of the party pointed to as evidence that the eyes had really been taken out, whereupon shouts were raised by the excited mob who were present, and loud cries of vengeance against the foreigners, not one of whom they vowed should be left alive. Fortunately, however, there were dissentients among themselves. One of the mandarins, a friend of Chung-How's, took the part of foreigners and declared that these exhumed remains proved nothing; while on the other hand a strong opponent of Chung-How's said they proved every thing against foreigners. The exploring party separated, leaving a very uneasy feeling on the minds of many of the spectators, and of some to whom the affair was reported.

Yesterday, the 10th, Tsêng-Kwo-Fan issued a proclamation in which he discredited the stories circulated against foreigners, and called on the people to respect the edict of the emperor, and be quiet, not to go down to the Settlement in numbers, nor without business, and not to interfere with foreigners coming to the city on business, &c. This proclamation calmed the minds of the respectable, but roused the ire of the more unruly portion of the people, who were so incensed that they cut it in pieces, saying "we expected him to lead us against foreigners, and lo! he turns foreigner himself." The well-to-do classes are however quite satisfied that all is now well, only they would have to pay some cash to soothe the French.

Two members of the British legation, Messrs. Frazer and Adkins, had visited Tientsin to investigate the recent occurrences. They had had an interview with Tsêng-Kwo-Fan, and are believed to be thoroughly satisfied that "all is well," that the ringleaders in the massacre will be duly punished by their own authorities without the intervention of either France or

England, which means that some mandarin will be degraded one step and in a few months be advanced two. With which peaceful massage they returned to the bosom of Mr. Wade and the Tsung-li yamên.

Nero fiddled while Rome burned.

No. 24.

PROCLAMATION BY TSENG-KWO-FAN, VICE-ROY OF CHIHLI, AT TIENTSIN.

July 10*th*, 1870.

Whereas with reference to the affair of the 13th day of the 5th moon (June 21st), I have received repeated decrees, commanding me equitably to investigate and take action in the matter, with the resolute design to give no opening for hostilities, it is the duty of all, whether servants of the State or simple subjects, to correspond to the intentions of His Majesty, making it their object to allay trouble and give tranquillity to the people. Accordingly, this proclamation is issued to the resident population in general. It is your duty to pursue, as before, your accustomed avocations, and you are forbidden to roam about the streets and form assemblages in numbers, spreading abroad unfounded rumours, mutually alarming and disturbing each other. Equally is it forbidden to collect together in the neighbourhood of the foreign houses and foreign vessels, thereby giving rise to occasions of quarrel. As regards the measures to be taken for inquiring into, and judicially dealing with, the affair in question, I shall as in duty bound hold a stringent investigation and arrive at a decision thereupon in conformity with the principles of justice, and shall show not the slightest partiality or negligence. Let all tremblingly obey &c.

No. 25.

TIENTSIN, 11*th July*, 1870.

To the Editor of the
"SHANGHAI EVENING COURIER."

SIR,—Self-defence is sometimes so apt to look like self-praise that were it not most important on other grounds for your readers to know the utter worthlessness of any of the statements of a certain *starred* Tientsin correspondent, we should allow the reckless charges he has brought against ourselves to pass unnoticed. As it is, we simply record the following facts as answering his reflections on our body in your issue of July 4th.

First.—The houses of the Protestant missionaries at Tientsin are in a more exposed position than at any other foreign residence not actually situated in the city. They stand nearest the point occupied by the chief actors in the recent horrible outrages as their principal rendezvous, and were thus in no small danger in case of an attack. The houses on the bund gave to their occupants the advantage of an immediate communication with the means of escape. The *Daily News* correspondent is supposed to be a gentleman whose own quarters are at the end of the Settlement furthest from the city, and it is not unlikely that this and *other* weighty considerations go far to account for his own professed tranquillity.

Secondly.—As one of the effects of "the friendly feeling of the people" towards us (many other having been forthcoming) we were duly apprised of the intention of an organised band of desperadoes to attack our houses for purposes of plunder, and were also informed of the often repeated declaration of the mob to destroy our English church, which is in close proximity to our dwellings. That this was no meaningless threat is proved by the fact that the writers caught a villain in the church tower, who admitted that he was intent on an incendiary act.

Thirdly.—Common sense, no less than the chivalry upon which our countrymen have been wont to pride themselves, demanded that in such a time of anxiety and peril, women and children should be placed, if possible, in a position of safety. Such a course was deemed necessary and urged upon us by many noble men amongst the gentlemen of the Tientsin community. This was held to be alike necessary for the calmness and security of the mothers and little ones, and for our own unfettered co-operation in such measures as might be decided upon for the public welfare.

Fourthly.—On the afternoon of the day of the massacre, the undersigned placed themselves at the disposal of the English consul, and those acting with him, to be used in any way that might be thought best for helping to meet the demands of the grave crisis in which we were involved. We offered either to take the sole responsibility of watching over our own outposts, or, if it were considered more important, to leave our dwellings and effects to the mercy of circumstances and take duty on the Settlement. We were told that the greatest service we could render to the general interest would be to remain at our own houses, and watch the approaches from the city. This responsibility we cheerfully accepted, and we say to your correspondent that it is *simply false* that we ever deserted our posts for one moment, or that we ever designed or desired to do such a cowardly thing. If your contemporary's correspondent had not been so absorbed in the preparation of his plausible, but dangerous articles, he might have seen for himself, what almost every other member of the community saw, that during those dark and dreadful nights in the early stage of this fearful drama, we were endeavouring to be second to none in vigilant watchfulness and hardy endurance. It is true that only two of us were to be found at the houses, but why was this? It is explained by the fact that one of our number who had just passed through a painful bereavement and was somewhat out of health, was encouraged to remain for a brief period on board the *Manchu,* while the other two members of our missionary circle were discharging their mission duties at far distant country stations. We therefore consider that the correspondent is bound to withdraw his unfounded assertions, or, failing this, to cease hurling his envenomed shafts from behind a screen, that the public, knowing the man, may know what value to set upon his testimony.

In conclusion, we remark that a three-fold motive actuated us in determining to continue on our mission premises. There was the one already referred to, as arising out of the knowledge that the ruffians were only waiting for our departure to plunder and burn our mission property, which achievement would assuredly have been the signal for a general rush upon the Settlement. Another consisted in the fact that we were thus in a position from our hourly intercourse with the people, to give the earliest and most reliable information respecting the state of feeling in the city. The last, and with us a very influential motive, was that thus we might cheer and strengthen our suffering converts. Though the correspondent can afford to despise the results of missionary labour in this place, *we* have no reason to regret our resolution to stand by the native christians to the last, and, whether Protestant or Roman, to render them every assistance in our power. Their urgent entreaties that we should care first

and chiefly for our own safety; their affectionate anxiety on behalf
of our families; their unshaken stedfastness in this terrible hour
of trial; the sorrow through which they have patiently passed,
amounting in not a few cases, literally, to "the loss of all things,"
and in others to cruel beatings and imprisonments, have endeared
them for ever to our hearts, and are indeed an all-sufficient answer
to the taunts that we have laboured nine years in the Tientsin
vineyard in vain.   Never did these men stand so high in our
estimation as now.   Some of them have proved very heroes.   We,
who knew them best, had never dared to hope that so much of
christian manliness had alredy been developed in our little churches.
And now, more than every secure of their confidence and love,
we can afford to laugh to scorn the sneers of an anonymous
writer, whose slur upon the courage and devotion of Protestant
missionaries, was only what might be expected from one who
could insinuate that our martyred Catholic sisters deserved their
cruel fate.   We are Sir, your obedient servants.

> WILLIAM N. HALL.
> JONATHAN LEES.

No. 26.

PEKING.

The American missionaries had a meeting here on the 5th to
consider the unsatisfactory information furnished by the American
consul at Tientsin to the minister, and if necessary to memorialise
Mr. Low and, possibly, the home government on the subject.
"Dr. Williams and Mr. Low," we are told, "only err from defec-
tive information.   Dr. Martin is all right.   He feels disappointed
and chagrined at the conduct of the Chinese government."   The
president of the Peking university is further understood to have
expressed himself favourable to a war which would awake the
Chinese out of their rottenness.   This is indeed a reaction from
Burlingamism of which the Professor of Hermeneutics has been
so conspicuous a partisan, but we have no doubt he is as sincere
now as on previous occasions when he has changed his opinions,
probably more so, as the present utterances bespeak a tendency
to return to his first love.

Chêng of the "Foreign Office," who is to succeed Chung-How, is still in Peking. He is said to be a "very good fellow," but timid about going to Tientsin.

The Roman Catholic priests are believed to have left town.

Three individuals have been seized, accused of kidnapping. Several children in the neighbourhood have disappeared, and few patients visit the foreign hospital. The feeling against foreigners is, if anything, increasing, but no danger is apprehended. All the ministers, except Mr. Wade, are in town.

The opinion of well-informed people in Peking is, that if the Tientsin business be slurred over, it will be impossible for foreigners to live in the north of China away from the sea.

No. 27.

NEWCHWANG.

July 12*th*, 1870.

Business is nearly at a stand-still. It was never worse, if ever so bad, before. The harbour is nearly empty of ships, and a few days ago there was not a single foreign vessel in port. When the *Kiushu* leaves, an hour hence, there will only be one foreign vessel in port.

Sycee is dearer than it was in winter. In the last few days the exchange has been considerably over twelve *teaous* per tael. There is so little sycee in the market, that it is not expected the exchange will fall much below the present rate, for some months.

About the 29th or 30th of last month, rumours of a massacre of foreigners at Tientsin reached us, through a Chinese source. These were at first not believed, the natives however evidently gave credit to the horrible story. The tale of horror was, that *all* the foreigners were murdered; and it was affirmed that it had been in contemplation, to treat all foreigners at Peking, Tientsin and Newchwang in the same manner. The natives here were very excited, and the Cantonese and southern Chinese generally, were in a state of great alarm. Foreigners were just beginning to think, there might possibly be a grain of truth in the Chinese reports, when on Sunday morning 3rd July, a North-German vessel (the *Emma*) arrived here from Taku. The captain had been at Tientsin and said he had seen the murdered body of the French consul, and heard the particulars of the cruel butchery of the Sisters of Mercy. It was now beyond a doubt, that a great and scandalous crime had been committed. Foreigners here became anxious, the report that a general massacre at Peking, Tientsin and Newchwang had been contemplated, obtained more or less credence; and now the foreigners equally with the Chinese were impressed with a sense of danger. Our community is a scattered one, the means of defence against a Chinese rising do not exist, there were only two sailing vessels in port, and not one gun-boat was near. It is not wonderful then that when the last foreign vessel left our port, we all more or less felt our position to be a perilous one, and that we were in a somewhat anxious state. We did not like the idea of having actually no ship to which, as a last resort, we might betake ourselves, or to which we might send our women and children. It was a great relief to every one when on Saturday morning (9th July) our deserted harbour was once more enlivened by the *Kiushu*, which brought the detailed account of the Tientsin tragedy, and the assurance that everything was quiet there. We are told moreover, that the Tientsin people (foreigners) take the massacre quietly, that the feeling is one of sympathy for this foul deed, but this is to us incredible. Whatever the practices of the French priests may be, nothing can justify so monstrous a murder, and it is to be hoped that the French government will in a signal and impressive manner, visit upon the Chinese government a righteous retribution. Unless this is done, we cannot hope to live in peace in China; and we shall be startled ere long by hearing of another catastrophe, greater in its magnitude at one or other of the ports, and without the slightest excuse which friends of the mandarins advance in extenuation of the Tientsin tragedy.

You will be astonished to learn that as yet no gun-boat has visited us. Living as we do in a place where there is only slight steam communication with the southern ports, one would naturally have expected our naval or consular authorities to send a gun-boat here, when they heard of the disturbance at Tientsin. But I suppose we must wait, until some of us get murdered. Surely if a gun-boat is needed anywhere, it is here, but that again may be a reason for not sending one.

The *Kiushu* starts for Shanghai *via* Chefoo about 11 a. m.

No. 28.

The following is an authentic report of evidence on the late massacre given by a respectable Chinaman at Tientsin :—

TIENTSIN, *July 4th*, 1870.

Evidence of———

The man———resides on the east of the river, the rendezvous of large numbers of the parties implicated in the recent violent outrages against foreigners.   He is a man of known integrity of character.   During the past fortnight, I have had several conversations with him, and have received from him voluntary testimony of which the following is an epitome :—

For some weeks before the outbreak witness had heard of a contemplated attack on the French church.   In the first instance, the rumours involved no reference to designs on the lives of foreigners, and the only motive assigned for the threatened destruction of property was, that the beneficial courses of the Feng Shui, which were considered to be seriously obstructed by its existence, might thereby be effectively restored.   It was only a few days before the attack that he heard of any intention to kill foreigners, and when this was first spoken of in his presence, the French residents—more commonly the called Tien Chu Chiau, or Roman Catholics, were alone mentioned as the victims to be sacrificed.   At this time the talk about Feng Shui had given place to wild stories respecting the alleged abduction by Romish emissaries of native children, and even of adult persons, who were said to have been put to death, and to have been used for various medical compositions and applications.   These absurd rumours were diligently and rapidly circulated, so that, at length, he found it impossible to go anywhere without hearing them adverted to. The cry then began to be raised "death to *all* foreigners and the entire demolition of foreign property."   On Sunday, the 19th of June, the members of the fire brigades in the locality of———'s residence appeared on the streets in great force, and ostentatiously published their hostility to foreigners and their deliberate decision to massacre the whole foreign population.   He did not think that this threat would be carried into execution, as he had heard such announcements in former years and knew they had not been verified; but be became so alarmed by manifestations around him that he retired from the neighbourhood, and, accompanied by his aged mother, made his way to some relations residing in the country. His friends advised him to remain with them until certain that the popular commotion had subsided, but, on Tuesday forenoon, 21st of June, he ventured to return to his home in the hope that the crisis was passed. When drawing near to the Ho-shen-mun, he observed that the main thoroughfares were thronged with armed men, and that the utmost disorder prevailed. He also heard oft repeated cries of "death to all foreign devils." Taking a circuitous route through comparatively unfrequented paths and alleys he shortly reached his own house, which stands some yards distant from the main street in that district. He ascended the roof of his dwelling for purposes of observation, and had scarcely taken his position there, when he saw the mob madly rushing towards three chairs, which were being hurriedly borne in the direction of the foreign Settlement. The chairs were seized within a stone's throw of his house, and the deafening cry was raised "here are foreigners! kill the foreigners." The rabble began to strike the chairs, and the occupants (the poor Russians) jumped out exclaiming "we are not French, we are English." He distinctly heard the reply "that does not matter, we will kill all." He saw the rioters seize a foreign lady, and strike her with their swords. Two foreign gentlemen attempted to rescue her, but they were immediately struck down, and, to all appearance, instantly killed. The lady was then subjected to brutal indignities. She was stripped of her clothing, her person was mutilated, a finger was cut off for the sake of her ring which she wore, and other barbarities perpetrated. The bodies of the lady and gentlemen were then taken and burned on the plain, but he afterwards heard that they were taken up at dark and thrown into the river. He noticed a number of yamên runners on the scene, but did not see a single official. These men never attempted to interfere with the proceedings of the mob except in one instance, when they advised that the foreign Settlement could not be attacked *on the day*. Their whole deportment was that of men who approved of the acts of the crowd. He solemnly declares that the guilty offenders claim the leading officials with the exception of Chung-Kung-Paou, as heartily encouraging this attack on foreigners. The last named official he pronounces to be in great disfavour with the people, because of his known disposition to save foreigners from these violent and murderous assaults. He testifies that up to yesterday, Sunday, July 3rd, thousands of men were parading the streets, armed, and eager to complete the extermination of foreigners, and that nothing but the arrival of gun-boats has prevented them from visiting the Settlement. He most confidently asserts that any foreigner going to the east of the river would be instantly killed, and he knows that the same thing holds good with regard to various parts of the city and its suburbs. He knows the rioters to be exultant at the approach of Tsêng-Kwo-Fan's troops, and to be constantly declaring that a large proportion of the soldiers are in sympathy with their hateful designs, and will unite with them in seeking their accomplishment. They parade the streets calling for volunteers to aid their dark crusade, and openly and loudly ask—"What of those gun-boats? The foreign devils are few, we are many, and even though some of us be killed, we can soon overcome them by force of numbers." As an incitement to co-operation, they remind the people that the deeds of 21st of June were followed by needed and abundant rain, and that this circumstance clearly indicates the will of Heaven to have them prosecute to its consummation the object on which they have set their hearts.

Other details were furnished by this witness, but the above paragraph comprizes the more important items of his calmly expressed testimony.

No. 29.

TIENTSIN.

July 14th, 1870.

Tsêng-Kwo-Fan has suspended three mandarins here; the footai Chu-Chia-Hün has been replaced by Tang-Shen-Chang; the che-fu Ching-Kwang-Tsao by Ma-Sheng-Wu; the che-hsien Liu-Chieh by Hsiao-Shih-Pen.

Tsêng-Kwo-Fan is about to send for troops to catch and punish the ringleaders in the late massacre. At Taku it is reported that shot and shell are being placed in the forts, and another port being opened by which the shipping in the first reach in the river on the landward side of the forts may be commanded by the guns of the forts.

Of Cheng-Lin, the successor appointed to Chung-How, it has
been already remarked that he is timid about coming to Tientsin,
and he is now reported "sick." It is a curious fact that the
mothers of several of the Peking teachers in Tientsin fell sick at
same the time, rendering it necessary for the teachers to visit
Peking whence they have not yet returned.

No. 30.

COUNCIL ROOM,
SHANGHAI, 18th *July*, 1870.

PRESENT:

G. B. Dixwell, Esq.—*Chairman*.
David Reid, Esq.—*Vice-Chairman*.
W. Cameron, Esq.
J. Anderson, Esq.
J. G. Purdon, Esq.
S. J. G. Jellicoe, Esq.
W. Remé, Esq.
T. Probst, Esq.
            Alex. J. Johnston—*Secretary*.

The minutes of the last meeting were confirmed and signed.
The following report from the defence committee was read and
adopted.

REPORT OF THE DEFENCE COMMITTEE.

Your committee have the pleasure of laying before you a report
of their proceedings.

Upon your deciding to accept the control of the Shanghai
Volunteer Corps, measures were taken for arming the Corps viz:
for the purchase from Messrs. Ilbert & Bidwell and Glover, Dow
& Co., of 500 stand of breach-loading rifles—Sneiders—with
100,000 rounds of ammunition, the necessary accoutrements, &c.

The rifles, by the terms of the contract entered into, are to be
delivered within a month from the date of the acceptance of the
tender.

Pending the arrival of these arms from Japan, Mr. Groom has
very kindly given your Committee the use of 500 short Enfield
rifles, with accoutrements.

They have been served out to the members of the three Rifle Companies and of the Shanghai Fire Brigade.

They will be withdrawn from the companies upon the issue of the Sneider rifles. To meet the present emergencies, your Committee have purchased 10,000 rounds of ammunition, a proportion of which has been served out with the short enfields.

The Mounted Rangers will be provided with breach-loading pistols, swords, &c., &c.

The purchase of these arms, your committee are glad to be able to state, has met with the almost unanimous approval of the Rate-payers.

Your committee have had two rifled 12 lbs. breach-loading guns placed at their disposal by the courtesy of Mr. Telge.

An application has been made to H. E. the Major-General commanding H. M.'s forces at Hongkong for the services of a qualified drill and musketry instructor to the Volunteers who arrived by the *Sunda*. In regard to placing the drill instructor, sergeant Chapman, at the disposal of the Volunteers, Major-General Whitfield observes "Sergeant Chapman is well suited for the duties he will be called upon to perform—he has not been at Hythe, but has gone through several courses of musketry with his company.

It affords me much pleasure to be enabled to comply with the request of the Council and to be in a position to offer this slight assistance to the Volunteer movements at Shanghai."

Your committee have conferred with the Hon. Capt. Denison of H. M.'s S. *Zebra*, and the officers commanding companies, in regard to defensive measures, and various points of detail affecting the corps.

The muster Sneider rifle has been tried by Captains Maclean, Cann and Kidner, who have handed your committee a very satisfactory report on it.

No. 31.

TIENTSIN.

Our advices from this quarter are not of a particularly satisfactory nature. There was a fear that the French Chargé d'Affaires had made a premature settlement of the tragedy of June 21st, the conditions being the rebuilding of the cathedral and hospital within the city as before, and of the consulate at Tzchulin (the foreign Settlement); two mandarins to be beheaded. Count Rochechouart is believed to have been "talked over" by certain infatuated persons to a belief in the Chinese versions of the Tientsin massacre, which are so palpably false that they need not deceive a baby. Chung-How has been acquitted of the murder, and the French representative has been hob-nobbing with him on the most familiar terms (greatly to the indignation, we are glad to learn, of the unsophisticated officers of the gun-boats) without even the pretence of an enquiry. Two mandarins are reported to be condemned to death, equally without anything approaching to a legal trial or such an investigation as would satisfy the least fastidious of civilized races. Money does the rest! But it seems more likely that M. Rochechouart is fooling the Chinese, rather than that he has forfeited the respect which his firm and consistent career previously had won for him.

To have two mandarins actually beheaded, and the fact notified in the *Peking Gazette* would of course be an important point from a political point of view. It will be curious to see how this is carried out; but however desirable it may be to dispense with what is technically called "war," the man holding the responsible position of Count Rochechouart, who would allow such an occasion to pass without taking precaution to prevent future outbreaks, without tracking the recent atrocities to their real authors (even if the Vice-Roy Tsêng-Kwo-fan, or higher power still, should be implicated) without settling once and for ever the wretched question of audience, and generally placing the Chinese in their true position, is no statesman.

Mr. consul Lay has been very energetic in collecting and sifting facts for the information of the British Chargé d'Affaires, the tenor of which was to criminate the Chinese authorities. The consular zeal has lately cooled down, owing, it is supposed, to the fact that Mr. Wade has become intolerant of information. From the first he is said to have decided that the massacre was an accidental street riot, and a street riot it shall remain.

On the attitude of the foreign representatives at Peking, a correspondent makes the following sensible observations:—

How like mockery it seems, to read of these gentlemen taking it comfortably at the hills, and taxing their ingenuity to make it appear that this hideous crime is a small affair. They can afford to smile at the reports sent them from Tientsin, to treat them as the frenzied ebullitions of a lot of alarmists, and to regard this fearful massacre as the freak of a suddenly excited populace. The butchery of 19 men and women, a month's loss of peace, the almost total suspension of trade, the demolition of nearly a score of buildings, the sacrifice of nobody knows how many natives, the perpetual clamourings of the lawless villains for the completion of their work of blood by the utter extermination of foreigners, and the damning evidence we have of the culpability of some of the officials in this enormous tragedy; all this fails to convince these gentlemen that there is much reason for complaint, or any cause for fear. Here is a grand opportunity for placing foreign relations with China on a more substantial and satisfactory basis than has ever been practicable; but let this chance pass without due improvement, and what may we next look for in the shape of indignity and humiliation.

No. 32.

TIENTSIN.

(From our Correspondent.)

July 18th, 1870.

Some of your readers may think it strange that no public expression of sympathy has been called forth from the Tientsin community on account of the late sad affair here. Our indignation has been deep and strong, and has been loudly and forcibly expressed among ourselves, both as to the cowardly miscreants who were the instigators and actors in the horrible tragedy, and also in regard to the unfortunate individual among ourselves who so far forgot himself and his nationality as to become their apologist.

The Sisters of Mercy were often among us and were highly respected by all who knew them, for their good deeds and self-sacrificing labours;—much deep sympathy is felt for them and for their friends.

The community felt it due to themselves to let the writer of communications from Tientsin which appeared in the *N. C. Daily News* of 28th June and 4th July over the signature *   *   *   * know how strongly they disapproved of those communications.

Who the writer was, was perfectly well known to every man and woman in the Settlement. To this individual a letter was therefore drawn up and signed by land-renters representing nearly every lot in the Settlement. But two respected members of the foreign community thought it well before that letter was sent, to send a written enquiry whether he acknowledged himself to be the writer of the two offensive communications. To this enquiry his answer was as follows:—"I beg leave to own receipt of your letter of yesterday's date asking me to give you information in respect to the writer of some letters which have lately appeared in the *N. C. Daily News*. In reply I beg to state that as I am neither the manager nor editor of the *N. C. Daily News*, I am not the proper person to apply to, but that you should direct your question to either of those gentlemen."

At the same time that this reply was received it was reported on good authority that Mr. John A. T. Meadows had acknowledged himself the author of the letters in question, and said he was sorry he had written them. The landrenters' letter was then sent to Mr. Meadows. It was as follows:—

JOHN A. T. MEADOWS, Esq.,
> *Chairman Municipal Council.*
>> Tientsin.

SIR,—We the undersigned land-renters and others residing at Tientsin, disapproving in the strongest manner of your conduct in the late most serious and sad affair here, and believing you to be, from your words and action here, the writer of articles in the *N. C. Daily News*, which we consider to be unjust and untrue, and calculated to damage, in the eyes of all good men, were such reports not contradicted—the reputation of the foreign residents here;—have to request that you will resign at once into the hands of the land-renters your office of Municipal Councillor.

(Signed by nine resident land renters, and by nine gentlemen residing here who approve of the same.)

To this Mr. Meadows replied:—"As I shall, as you have no doubt already heard, very soon take my departure from Tientsin, and as I shall in these circumstances, not be here to attend to my duties as one of the Municipal Councillors, I resolved some days back to send in my resignation to you on the afternoon of this day. I now therefore carry out that intention and have now to request you will please communicate my resignation to our colleague Mr. Hannen for his information. I am in receipt of a letter from the land-renters and it is my intention to reply to it during the next 18 days."

More than enough of your space being now occupied by the above affair, I turn to the general news.

Count Rochechouart and most of his staff arrived here yesterday from Peking, having visited their Excellencies Tsêng-Kwo-Fan and Chung-How on his way down. He has also visited the scene of the massacre. This morning Chung-How is reported to have taken breakfast with him on board the *Flamme* where he has taken up his quarters. He has also received the cards of some smaller mandarins. It is said the officers of the French steamer are very much annoyed at his conduct, and think he is allowing himself to be talked over to the British and American way of settling things. I rather think he may be borrowing a leaf of Chinese etiquette and playing with them until he is able to work. One or two gentlemen remain at the French legation in Peking. Three priests came down with the party and it is said they have been ordered by Rochechouart to return to their chapels and their work. They replied their chapels were all destroyed. He then told them to put up mat-roofs, but they said they would not go up to the city without a gun-boat. Is all this a little by-play to throw dust in the eyes of the Chinese?

As to the British Legation, Mr. Lay our consul here, collected and forwarded to Mr. Wade an immense mass of evidence criminating the Chinese authorities; but of late no more has been asked for or sent. Both the British and American chiefs seem to pray: "give peace in our time." The letter sent in to the Tsungli yamên on the news of the massacre was strongly worded in the original; this, however, the British minister would not sign; he got it to translate into Chinese and then made it so that he could sign it.

The gentleman mentioned in your paper of 9th July was deserted at Tsinanfoo by all his servants and had to take refuge in the house of two priests some distance off. The people were threatening to kill all foreigners as has been done at Tien-tsin. The lives of some foreign merchants at Tien-tsin were saved by a banker, a chemist, and some compradores, whose houses line the lane leading to the Settlement, and who stopped the crowd as they came rushing on by assuring them that all the foreigners had fled.

I heard the other day of another apologist for the assassins. He also is in the Chinese Imperial service. It is well to hear both sides of the question. H. E. Chung-How will not be condemned without a fair trial, and if he can be proved innocent all must rejoice. But on the other hand a soldier who shows the white feather in action may be shot at once, and what then ought to be the fate of a general like Chung-How who through cowardice even, allows an army of martyrs to be sacrificed? A few days before the massacre the Sisters said that up to within a week of that time the mandarins always said they did not believe the stories current against them. But about the time mentioned they received a letter from the mandarins which insinuated that these were beginning to be believed. In one of the *Cycles* I believe it is said that a post-mortem examination had taken place at the Sisters' hospital lately. Careful enquiry justifies me in contradicting that statement. No such examination has taken place in the Catholic establishment within the experience of any medical man here. The river between this and Taku is still considered unsafe for foreigners; several have been threatened and some in great danger. Now that the Catholic priests have come down we hope to get the evidence of their converts.

The other day an old servant, now second in command of a recently built steamer, called, and in talking matters over he said the mandarins all denied complicity. I said if they had been innocent, why did Tseng-Kwo-Fan degrade some of them? He quickly answered that that went for nothing. The mandarins of a place where trouble arose were always punished whether guilty or not. The British Chargé d'Affaires will be satisfied if the Chinese punish the offenders. The punishment will be as usual— the loss of a button and removal to a higher station.

When, like the British Minister, you get tired of hearing about these things please let me know, and I will write no more till the fighting begins. Yours truly,

---

No. 33.

The following letter from a missionary at Tientsin to a friend gives a very distinct idea of the state of feeling towards foreigners and their converts in the country for a considerable distance around

Tientsin. We are glad, however, to learn that his missing friends
have arrived overland at Chefoo:—

The messenger returned a few days ago, having traced————
as far as Tsinanfu, where he concluded that it would be fruitless
to continue pursuit any longer. He was obliged to take a circuitous route in returning, as he found the people on the main
roads full of deadly hatred to foreigners, and threatening harm to
all connected with the abominated barbarians. He of course can
testify to the state of feeling only on this side of Tsinanfu. Being
well known throughout this district as one of our most trusted
men, he was specially exposed to suspicion and danger. He says
————could not have passed through some of the places without
injury; but he thinks he might have got through by selecting
unfrequented lines of road. A messenger was sent to me by one
of our well-to-do members in Shantung, with kind enquiries after
my state and prospects. The messenger was so alarmed by the
demonstrations he encountered that he lost courage, and before I
could finish my reply to my Shantung friend, he had bolted, so
anxious was he to get home again.

The three girls whose abduction by the mob on the day of the
massacre caused me such horrible anxiety, were after much trouble
found and restored to us. A week ago I sent them away to their
distant homes in charge of two of their fathers and their old teachers.
The carter has returned to me, stripped of everything, and suffering from cruel beatings. The poor girls and their friends were
ill-treated by the people, who charged them with being sent in
charge of some rascally yamên runners to Lauling-hsien, which
means that they will be kept in prison till some of their poverty-
stricken relations raise a good sum for their ransom. The report
has been raised in some places that Mr. and Mrs. H. also secured
children for the vile purposes attributed to the Sisters. I am
distressed at this affair and propose to send another messenger off
at once to ascertain the present aspect of the case. A sum of
mission money was in the cart, but not a serious amount.

Some of the villains over the river have erroneously fancied that
I could bring some influence to bear on the French, and that it
might be worth while to conciliate me. Who they are I do not
know, but they sent a message to me the other day to the effect,
that if I would go and talk with them, they would protect me,
and that if I would promise to speak to the French in their favour,
they would restore some of the things stolen from our members.

I replied I had not a particle of influence with the French, and if I had such influence, it would not be used in their favour. They are said to be rapidly losing their bravery, and to be gradually clearing out. I suppose that by the time they are specially wanted none of them will be found.

No. 34.

We have been favoured with the perusal of a letter written from Peking to a friend, from which we make the following selections.

PEKING, 12th July, 1870.

Five minutes funk for their own wives aud babies would do more to convert Wade and Low than all the wisdom and truth you could uncover during the remainder of your lifetime. At present they are safe at "the hills" from any Peking attack. In this Tientsin affair we should strenuously contend against the misnomer "mob" or "riot" that it is tried to fasten to it. *Massacre* it surely was, and nothing else. I am told the guilds went in from Pukow, 35 *li* from Tientsin early on Tuesday morning *to be in time* for the attack. This I know for certain, and the same is said of other places within a 40 *li* redius. A foreigner's teacher came in a day or two ago from the S. W. and he says no foreign mission work can be done now. Those he went to baptize refused to come forward during this excitement. A friend, learned in such matters, believes the yamen *originate* the kidnapping stories. They force poor wretches to confess, who are then safely kept, or *safely killed* where the headless trunk cannot complain of unjust punishment.

As to the Mahommedan origin of these troubles, I hold, that either the Mahommedans, as being better organised, have been made use of just now by the Peking government, working through such officers as Tseng-Kwo-Fan; or, (and this I more incline to) the movement is really Mahommedan, who are bound to have a quarrel with some or all outsiders, with the French if that will only weaken the Chinese government without killing it; and if the French wont fight, they will kill off another batch. Perhaps the state of feeling south of Tientsin will throw new light on Williamson's death. At all events large pecuniary compensation for his widow ought to be recovered in connection with this Tien-

tsin affair. I cannot but hope, that the whole thing will lead
to the burial of the present 7 by 9 effete and worm-eaten representation of Old England at Peking. I assure you it will be
attended with few tears, and the funeral expenses will be paid
with pleasure. It is refreshing after seeing the conduct of the
English minister, to contrast with it the hard manly work, yes,
overwork, of the Tientsin consul. Do you know what is the great
passport to favour with Wade? Rip open your necktie; gasp for
breath; choke out a "Heaven take the missionaries who think
they know a diplomats' pidgin better than he does himself, placed
at a *cool observing distance*," and you have, I fancy, the key. You
ought to know that when a man's ideas are set in a cast-steel
mould, to add to those ideas is to burst the mould altogether. If,
therefore, any are so ill-advised as to send to Mr. Wade any more
implications of the high-minded Chinese officials, his ear drum,
ringing already with the foul calumny that mandarins have had to
do with this little eccentricity of an "outraged populace," that ear
drum will burst, and Wade be for ever deaf to all calls whether
human, diabolic, or missionary. A lady here says that in all this
"she sees nothing new."

The only thing that seems to keep most people here is the shame
of being the first to go. Let the panic become a little stronger
and all missionary ladies and children will be sent to Tientsin.
Dr. Dudgeon believes every place in Peking less safe than his
hall of health, conscious of a life generously spent for some of
these yellow skins, he meets suggestions of danger from Chinese,
as if people meant that his *old patients* were going to attack him.
These people won't understand that there are Chinese and Chinese;
foolish, ignorant, prejudiced, thick-heads on the one hand, and
on the other the scum of creation, hireling villanous cut-throats,
sure of reward even if their lives are sacrificed after perjuring
away the reputation of their foreign benefactors.

We hear that the French have no available foreign troops at
Saigon. That would postpone any action on their part till October
—almost too late in the season. On the other hand the Chinese
have it that there are 2,000 English troops at Tientsin. Thus
are a dozen or two of the marines magnified. But let the hand-
ful of marines withdraw, and the "2,000 troops" will appear as
having "fled" or been "all slaughtered." Mongol troops are
reported as coming down from their native haunts. The Chinese
have a just dread of these "meat eaters" themselves, and think

the very mention of them enough to frighten the French. But the French declaration of war might easily be a week in Peking before being known to the other legations; and a well informed official here says distinctly that the French will not pass this matter over lightly. Meantime it is apparently certain that France will have all to do: I have not heard what Russia will do. She can get satisfaction by a stroke of the pen as easily as to order 10,000 men round from 42° 50′ north lat. I doubt whether she will fight. If she does, it will probably be a case of partition, say making the Yangtse common and a boundary.

How blind the English speaking legations are! Civilization and humanity have never hesitated between the cry of the English colonist and the American Tartar. It will not hesitate now between Christian and Asiatic, but will heartily say "go on!" should France and Russia decide:—"We will ourselves see that your officials throughout the empire do no more of this horrible work. They will hereafter report to us alone. Retire upon what we leave you—bare life and living in Manchuria." England and America and Prussia, the great Protestant powers cannot deny the Romish and Greek Catholics leave to improve the people; and if they improve them off the face of the earth, as the Americans have done *their* Tartars, and as the corn cared for, always does the weed,—as the right always does the wrong, all the world will be as well pleased as they are to-day that English speakers think were Indian fishers smoked.

No. 35.

Chen-Kwo-Jui came north with an escort of 2,000. Everybody understood that he came for our extermination; for be it remembered that 2,000 troops dribbling ostentatiously through Shantung for 10 days would make a great impression. Their incendiary proclamations thus needed little planning. The emperor's edict counts for a *double entendre* to stave off time. The "seat of the trouble" is that these scribbling diplomatists wrote five days after the massacre saying it was "all over and a purely accidental mob," and the account cannot now be re-opened except at the expense of this pen-birth. So if you find anything new, no matter how important, remember that so far as Peking is concerned, the debit side is closed.

We have been amused by several caricatures.

Martin has been represented with his head under his arm, hat in left hand, waiting at the door of the U. S. legation, sending in his card, inscribed with his immortal sentiments at the American meeting of 5th July, on the situation. "I should be in favour of waiting till I had a case. In asking for protection, it adds to one's position to have a tangible and material grievance for which to ask definite redress. It could be far easier for Mr. Low to recover for our loss of life or property when a definite case is submitted to him for his aid." Another cartoon contains 16 coffins in progress from Trieste to Paris one week ahead of Chung-How and Meadows. Another represents a grave as deep as Etna's passions have rolled out in 20 centuries; all Burlingame's "shining crosses" in the liquid fire; the spitting fury of Asiatic devilishness at bottom. Martin's International Law above the lava enough to fill the crater," all about the crater arms and legs, burned and boiled, children smothered, Sisters ravished, dirks, swords, spears, guns, and above all, some of Meadows' new light field pieces, defending the black and red flag of this most pious government from the assaults of Frenchmen, who would climb to the throats of these wretches, not honoring them with a death of powder and ball.— Yours ever for the truth and the right, and for the future of both.

P. S.—The Chinese say some mandarins are afraid to go home at nights, and sleep in their yamêns. I feel more secure now having settled my line of action in case of trouble, viz: as *bee* a line out of Peking as the presence of women needing assistance will allow. But I expect our servants will leave us before we need to get on the move. It is objected to the theory of the Mahomedans having anything to do with the massacre, that———had a Mahomedan convert to Christianity, and yet the whole force of the outbreak was not employed to kill the renegade. It is objected by budding diplomatists doing a little virgin cross-examination that as the man caught in the Protestant church at Peking was not groaning under 144 gross of Bryant and May's patent safety matches (*Light only on the Box*) the story of incendiarism is only another figment of the disordered stomachs (no legation student, with the fear of Wade before his eyes will allow *any* missionary *any* brains at all) of Lees Missionaries & Co.

We consider Tsêng-Kwo-Fan's conduct the worst feature of all; taking up the French cemetery instead of the cut-throats; rifling a graveyard to urge on a mob instead of seizing the ringleaders to quiet Tientsin. He is reported to have returned to Pautingfoo immediately. 50 or 60 tons of munitions of war were brought into the city on the eve of the 12th. They are removing them from Meadows' Arsenal to Tungchow, and thence to Peking. The packages all showed foreign superintendence. It is reported here that Chung-How is eating gold leaf. Hart's boy is very sick. The children have left the Sisters here, whether sent or taken away, I cannot say. The mandarins have assured the Sisters that they are specially charged to keep them safe from harm.

Sister Louise, a british subject (*british* you observe with a small *b* as long as Williamson sleeps unavenged) will get as much thought of by these diplomatists, as the poorest thing that ever sinned and died. That's *English* representation at Peking. I am glad to see everybody jumping on Meadows. I mistake the great English heart, if her representative at Peking does not get the same treatment from the high beating heart of old England, when she hears that even under the instructions of the manly consul at Tientsin, he will not learn that there are times when outraged humanity makes ordinary ever-day selfishness a gallow's crime.

No. 36.

(From our Correspondent.)

TIENTSIN, 20*th July,* 1870.

I HEAR on good authority that since Mr. Wade has learned that Sister Louise was a British subject, he has taken up the question warmly and has written home about it. When the Chinese notice this fact it may serve as a hint to them, if they want a fight, as some say, to commence next time at one of the larger Legations; then possibly the Governments may be tempted to take some action in the matter.

A gentleman who made M. Rochechouart's acquaintance when he was south last year, called on him on board the *Flamme* the other day. Rochechouart said he believed Tseng-Kwo-fan to be an honest upright man, and one who would always be found when wanted. He was reminded of what was said of his anti-foreign proclivities, and that wherever he had been, trouble to foreigners had followed. He still declared he *did not* believe him guilty in the present case, nor Chung-How either. The latter he said had had no power to act, and all those under him were against him. He therefore wanted all those under Chung-How punished; the remains of the Sisters buried with great pomp on the site of the old Consulate, with a monument over them in a clear open space which might be seen in all coming time; the Cathedral and Sisters' Hospital re-built and put in the same state as formerly. These things he said were settled for, what else would be wanted he would not know until he heard from home. Chung-How was to proceed to France, and on his return was to be be accompanied by a Frenchman who would protect him and who would remain in China to see the terms of the agreement carried out. It is said Mr. Meadows is not to accompany Chung-How. He had called on Rochechouart who refused to receive him.

The French and British Admirals are both at Chefoo waiting instructions. Rochechouart did not telegraph at any length till the 26th and does not expect instructions for a fortnight yet. The first telegram by Grants' left here on the 22nd, and the first telegrams which arrive may bring an acknowledgment of their receipt at home, it being now 29 days since the massacre.

There were 10 Sisters murdered, but only 5 bodies have been recovered. It will be impossible,—at all events it will be a very unpleasant operation, to remove the bodies from their present resting place; and if removed many residents will be prevented from joining the funeral cortege who wish to do so; and this again will be misunderstood by the Chinese. They talk about putting the present coffins into others larger and stronger. Why, some of the present ones are 9 feet long and 4 feet broad and high! They are apparently impatient to have a grand ceremony.

Mr. Lay British and French Consul here applied to the Chinese Government for a guard to send to Tsi-nan-foo for Mr. Sandrie, a French subject. A guard of 45 men and a colonel was granted, with a letter to the Governor-General of Shantung for permission to convey Mr. Sandrie back. He is the gentleman whose servants ran away from him, and who was threatened with death.

The Russian authorities are said to be convinced that the murder of their three subjects was an accident, they having been mistaken for French. They are therefore said to intend no action in the matter.

If this affair is to be patched up in the manner indicated in such rumours as the above, it will show the absolute necessity of having the telegraph brought to the door of the Legations where there may be incompetent or timid ministers, so that instructions may be received from home at once on any emergency. And having the telegraph we may do without these expensive Legations altogether. Commend the matter to the Chancellor of the Exchequer. A great saving would doubtless be effected by the change.

At present the Chinese believe that France will be afraid to declare war on account of the danger in which it would involve the 300 French priests in China. Chung-How ought to have a fair, but searching trial as to his complicity or non-complicity in this matter; and if found guiltless so much the better for him. At present heaven and earth are being moved to bring him in "Not guilty," without the facts of the case being at all known; and on the other hand, all under him are considered guilty, without any extenuating circumstance being allowed in their favour.

This is the latest phase of the situation, and apparently a far from satisfactory one. It behoves your journalists to watch it narrowly, and to give forth no uncertain sound on the issues involved.

No. 37.

TIENTSIN.

The *Chihli* which arrived from the north to-day did not bring our usual correspondence, that having been put on board the *Manchu* which was detained at Chefoo taking in cargo. But we learn, on what seems reliable authority, that the *Manchu* brought on word to Chefoo that Rochechouart had at length begun to lay aside the garb of the mere diplomatist, and to adopt a course of vigorous action.

His first demand seems to have been that certain native Christian converts, who were known to be imprisoned in or near the city of Tientsin, should be brought alongside the *Flamme* within a given hour. He then demanded that Tseng-kwo-fan should visit him on board the *Flamme*, and finally, he demanded that the heads of the Chih-fu, the Chih-hsien and Tseng-kwo-fan's Lieutenant-General (Cheng-kwo-jui?) should be brought to him by a certain time. The alternative in each case was the bombardment of the city.

In compliance with the first demand, the native converts were brought alongside the *Flamme*, half-an-hour before the appointed time had expired.   The gentleman who told our informant alleged that he was an eye-witness of the ghastly spectacle which these poor persecuted wretches presented.   Their ears squeezed to pieces between slips of bamboo; their eye-lashes cut off; their knees dislocated; their whole body bearing evidence of the fiendish ingenuity and cruelty that had been used to wring from them something to support the anti-foreign mania of their persecutors   It will be remembered that this representation is corroborated by the statement of one of our recent letters from Tientsin, that it was known that a number of Christian converts were being tortured in prison.

Tseng-kwo-fan visited Rochechouart on board the *Flamme* with remarkable punctuality to the time mentioned.   He was willing to deliver up the heads of the Chih-fu and Chih-hsien; but he refused to allow his Lieutenant to suffer.   Whether he will persist in this refusal to the extent of subjecting the city to the dreadful ordeal of a bombardment, or whether Rochechouart will persevere in carrying out his ultimatum to the letter, remains to be seen. An unexplained point is whether this action of Rochechouart implies that he has been fortified and guided by telegraphic instructions from France or consultation with the Admiral at Chefoo.   It was thought not unlikely at Tientsin, that the Chinese would man Taku forts and shut in the French, who are already up the river.

No. 38.

SHANGHAI.

RUMOURS as to the state of affairs to-day are somewhat confused. It seems a well authenticated fact that Capt. Winstanley and his foreign assistants at the Chinese training camp of Feng-wen-shan are leaving, and returning to Shanghai, some of them indeed are said to be already here.   We have as yet had no explanation as to the cause, though the fact has not a re-assuring look.   Chinese rumour reports that 2,000 troops are on the march from Soochow for Shanghai.   Emissaries from the Taotai visited the settlement yesterday, apparently with the purpose of ascertaining the exact force, operations, and objects of our Volunteer movement. They also expressed a wish that our military demonstrations should be given up as having a tendency to unsettle the public mind. It is said on the other hand that Monday is the day agreed on for a rising of the Chinese against our Settlement; though with such a force as we can now muster ashore, and such a powerful flotilla as we can lay abreast of their unarmed city walls we can hardly imagine men so insane as to provoke a conflict. Besides the tone of the proclamations by the Viceroy and the Taotai, translations of which we give elsewhere, and which have been freely posted and much perused throughout the City and Settlement, is of a re-assuring kind, and the whole action of our local authorities has every appearance of loyalty;—and is indicative, in fact, of apprehension rather than of menace. The wild talk of the tea shops has been evidently restrained, partly in consequence of the proclamations, but partly also we are told, in consequence of two tea-shop politicians having been soundly flogged for not controlling their utterances regarding existing difficulties. We hear that the North-German frigate *Hertha* with her hundreds of hardy tars, and her heavy armament, will probably soon be added to the fleet at Shanghai. We may well therefore feel that there is nothing in the whole aspect of things to disturb our attitude of calm preparedness.

No. 39.

LETTER TO "SHANGHAI EVENING COURIER."

DEAR SIR,—The following is the substance of a conversation which took place yesterday in the city between myself and a respectable Chinaman, as to the present aspect of affairs consequent upon the late massacre. A. is myself, B. the Chinese gentleman;

B. What about Tientsin affairs?

A. Nothing decided yet. The French community are waiting for orders from their Emperor.

B. What do *you* think will the Emperor say?

A. I have no idea.

B. If the French allow this matter to pass unnoticed, they will lose face amongst the Chinese.

A. What then do you think the best thing to be done?

B. Why, of course, to kill Chung-how!

A. But, people say that he is favourable to foreigners.

B. Ah! It is well known that he received a despatch from the Footai ordering him to investigate the rumours current amongst the people about the missionaries, before the massacre took place; but he threw that despatch on one side, and would not inquire into the matter. If he had attended to his orders, the massacre could not, by any means, have taken place. The French ought to kill him, otherwise this matter can never be settled. If they allow him to escape, then all men will despise them, and more murders will take place.

So far as I can discover, there seems to be a general impression amongst the people in the city, that the mandarins are to blame for not preventing the late massacre.—Yours truly,

OUTIS.

No. 40.

CHINKIANG.

SOME uneasiness is apparent at this port and placards against kidnapping and the "Paper man" are again posted on the walls. Reports of an intended pillage of Messrs. Russell & Co.'s Hulk, the *Governor General*, induced Captain Dunlop of the *Dove* to send a body of men on board on Saturday night, the junk men, of whom there are a number in the neighbourhood, being the suspected parties. No disturbance took place, however, but, in consequence of representations to the American Consul by the Chinese officials, who declared themselves unable to protect Frenchmen against whom the people were said to be much irritated, Mr. Blancheton of the Customs, who was the only French subject at the port except missionaries, was advised to leave rather than risk bringing on a riot, and this gentleman therefore proceeded to Shanghai by the *Plymouth Rock*.

No. 41.

CHENG-KWO-SHWAI.

THE above would be the spelling of the name 陳 國 瑞 according to Morrison's system, according to Wade's it would be Cheng-kwo-shuai. It has been commonly written Ching-kwo-jui. The individual bearing this name is that lieutenant-general of Tseng-kwo-fan, who within the last few weeks has acquired a bad pre-eminence among the Tientsin murderers, as having led on the fire-guilds who attacked the hospital of the Sisters of Mercy.

From what appears to be a perfectly reliable Chinese source we have obtained the following particulars of his antecedents. He is a native of Hûpeh and of a temperament essentially enthusiastic. In his opening manhood he had serious thoughts of retiring from the world into monastic seclusion; but hesitating between the Buddhists and the Taouists, who each strove with jealous rivalry to secure him, he became disgusted with their squabbles, and threw himself with all the energy of his character into the vortex of political agitation. He was adopted by the celebrated Chinese General San-ko-lin-sin, and during the war with England 1859 —1860 proved himself the ablest of his lieutenants. Since then he has been actively engaged in subduing and extirpating the Nienfei of Honan. Latterly he lived for a considerable time in or near Yangchow, and, undoubtedly, was at the bottom of the quasi-religious troubles which took place there two years (Sept. 1868) ago. He had previously boasted that he would give the foreigners a lesson they would remember. The humiliation to which that city was subjected as the result of those troubles, joined to the character he has everywhere acquired as a reckless agitator, makes the Yangchowites view with apprehension the probability of his return to them. A mansion still remains hired for his use. When the Mahomedan successes were becoming very numerous in Shensi and Shanse in the beginning of the year, he was called by Li-kung-pao, the generalissimo, to accompany him and take a command. He left Yangchow recently and visited Tseng-kwo-fan at Pau-ting-foo.

We cannot refrain from expressing a hope that the issue of the Tientsin investigations may be to relieve the good folks of Yang-chow once and for ever of any chance of his return. But such is his influence with Tseng-kwo-fan and the other magnates of the Chinese party, that our informant declares that the Manchu government dare not give him up to deserved punishment. The public sentiment will force them to fight rather than do so. Nothing but a defeat so disastrous as to imply an overwhelming necessity, would reconcile the Chinese to such a measure.

No. 42.

THE CHRISTIAN PRISONERS AT TIENTSIN.

The following account of the treatment of the Christian prisoners by the mandarins at Tientsin is on the authority of an eye-witness who has seen and personally examined them since their release. So much care has been taken to avoid over-statement that, as we have reason to know from other sources, the narrative falls short of the whole truth.

There were 45 or 50 Christians arrested at the time of the massacre many of whom made their escape or were released on the same day through the intervention of friends and acquaintances. Those who were actually incarcerated at the office of the City Magistrate were 15, 8 men and 7 women, details as follows:—

1. The first was gate-keeper. He was an old man of 65 and had a white beard. In spite of his age he was dragged through the streets and beaten almost till his flesh mortified. At the Che-hsien's yamên he was so maltreated that gangrene made its appearance; he has now eight serious wounds and his life is despaired of.

2. The gate-keeper of the Sisters, who was beaten, dragged through the dirt, and flung into the river, when he was taken to the yamên and put in irons without respect to his age. After the lapse of a month the running sores caused by the chains are still to be seen. The man is also suffering from 6 or 7 other wounds more or less serious, but his life is not in danger.

3. A christian from the country who had arrived on the morning of the 21st June. Having boldly confessed his faith he was put on the rack, made to kneel on chains, received 200 blows of the bamboo and was finally burnt on the back with red hot irons. His wounds are also visible, but nearly cicatrised. Their number bear eloquent testimony to the rage of the mandarins and the executioners.

4. Another christian from the country, subjected to treatment similar to the preceding.

5. A poor creature who was so drawn on the rack that his right foot is in a horrible state, more than thrice its natural size. Gangrene has set in, and maggots may be seen in an enormous cavity which has been formed. The doctor has decided that amputation is necessary to save this man's life.

6. The famous *Wang-sang*, arrested a little before the massacre as a sorcerer. Like all the rest he was accused of selling the hearts and eyes of children. It was the arrest of this man, in fact which constituted the first act in the little drama of the 21st June. Tortured like all the others, like them also he persisted to the end in affirming that all the calumnies against the Sisters of Charity were nothing but absurd and senseless lies. His beard has been plucked out. He is still so terrified at the dreadful sufferings he has been made to undergo, that he is like a person who has lost his reason.

7 and 8. Were not known to have been imprisoned until now; they are still at the yamên. The name of one is unknown; the other is the brave fellow who did not fear to throw a stone into the chair of the Chi-fu while he was exciting the people to the carnage, and who asked him "Why do you burn our church and massacre our fathers and our sisters!"

The first six christian confessors of the faith were released on the 22nd July; and the mandarins, who ought at least to try to appease the anger of the Europeans and sooth the pains of these unfortunate people, were not ashamed to send them back without any kind of clothing, or with only a rag of cloth to cover their nakedness, and that after having left them 24 hours without food!

The female prisoners are seven in number, all taken at the house of the sisters.

The first was assistant in their pharmacy, a widow of about 35. She also was conducted to the yamên of the Che-hsien, was cruelly beaten and thrown into a dungeon.

The remaining five, young girls of 18 to 22 years, were led to another place called Shoo-fan. Alas! it is known too surely that place had more horrors for them than the prison itself, and that they there, in all probability, lost by force what was dearer to them than life itself. Unhappily in spite of all efforts, and all entreaties of the French fathers, and all the eager promises of the new mandarins, these poor girls have not yet been given up to their families.

As for the 141 children from the orphanage of the Sisters, they also are in the hands of the mandarins; but it is hoped they will soon be released.

An English doctor who likewise had an opportunity of examining some of the prisoners, thus describes their state :—

"At the request of the French Minister 4 Roman Catholic converts have been removed from the yamên to the foreign Settlement.

One is an old man over 60 years. They have all been more or less tortured in various ways, and present a perfectly horrible appearance; their bodies fearfully emaciated and covered with gangrenous sores, filled with maggots. One man has been placed on a rack, and all his joints cracked. Another has been beaten so severely on the hands and feet that the tendons are exposed.

There are still in the yamên 3 men and 6 women, (converts) but they are in such a wretched state that the authorities dare not move them. One of these women has had needles driven underneath her finger nails, and her body sprinkled over with drops of boiling oil. Another, a young girl aged 16 years, has had all her fingers chopped off by small pieces.

It is reported that they have suffered other indignities too horrible for publication."

No. 43.

H. B. M. Consulate,
Tientsin 20th July, 1870.

Sir,—I have been requested by H. B. M.'s Chargé d'Affaires, to ascertain the amount of damage sustained by British subjects during the late unfortunate troubles.

As I am aware that many of your chapels were destroyed, and much valuable property lost, I have to request you, if you see fit, to have estimates made of the losses and send them to me, in order that they may be forwarded to the Chinese authorities.

Your obedient Servant,

W. H. Lay,
Acting Consul.

Reply of Messrs. Lees and Hall to the foregoing Communication.

Tientsin, 21st July, 1870.

Sir,—We have the honour to acknowledge the receipt of your official letter to us, dated the 20th instant, touching the losses sustained by the missions we represent, during the recent outrages.

We cannot but express our surprise, not only that at this early stage we should be required to state the amount of those losses, but that, prior to the settlement of the more important questions which are still pending, the subject of monetary compensation should be entertained at all.

Apart altogether from the fact that we are yet uncertain as to the action which will be taken at the present crisis,—almost certainly by the French, and possibly even by our own government —action which it might be as useless as it would be impolitic for us to forestall by consenting to any unsatisfactory condonation of the crimes which have been committed; it can hardly be necessary to remind you that until peace has been definitely secured, there are various items of loss for which we should feel it to be our duty to claim compensation, the limits of which can hardly yet have been reached. Such is the utter disorganisation of this city and neighbourhood, that all mission work must, in all likelihood, be suspended for months to come. Our respective staffs are thus thrown upon our hand. Our country converts, both in this province and in Shantung, are everywhere expecting new outbreaks, in their various districts. Native christians in the city continue to be daily exposed to spoliation and personal injury, while there is every reason to fear that our own appearance in the streets would still be fraught with danger.

With respect to our chapels, we fear that, however willing we might be to meet the wishes of His Excellency it is not possible for us to do so. Our converts hardly dare linger in the neighbourhood of the ruins; what hope can there be, then, that we can visit them in safety, or procure builders' estimates as to the cost of re-erection, not to speak of any actual attempt at restoration? Our deliberate conviction is, that such an attempt would only end in their renewed destruction, even if workmen could be found brave enough to undertake the task.

Will you forgive our expressing an anxious desire, not to be separated from our suffering French brethren, in any settlement of these unhappy troubles? This is not a mere question of sentiment. We cannot but feel that the interests of our country are involved in what has occurred. We are British subjects, resident here under the protection of treaties, and engaged in the prudent prosecution of our lawful calling. Our lives have been sought, our property has been destroyed, our converts grievously injured, and our characters assailed. Moreover, there seems good reason to believe, that at least one of the murdered Sisters was a British subject. There cannot be the slightest doubt in the mind of any one who has been brought much into converse with the people, during the last few weeks, that the original design was to treat all nationalities alike. It is easy to understand why the mandarins are now anxious to produce a different impression. But just as the excuses which unhappily served them so well, in regard to the outrages at Formosa, Yangchow, and elsewhere, fail them now, so should the evident falsity of their present professions of special friendship with ourselves, fail to separate us from those allies with whose interests our own so evidently are bound up.

We beg you will not mistake us. We are not crying for war and vengeance, but we do claim justice, and we hold most firmly to the belief, that the path of safety and of honour, no less for individual Englishmen than for our government, is to stand by our fellow-sufferers in the hour of trial. Nay, more, we believe this, for obvious reasons, to be the most merciful line of action in reference to the Chinese themselves.

We scarcely know whether we ought to apologise for venturing to express such views, for we hope that they find an echo in your own and every other heart. We have only, therefore, respectfully to assure you that we shall strive to meet, as soon as possible, the wishes of H. B. M. Chargé d'Affaires, and request you to represent to him our difficulties in the matter. We are, Sir,

Your most obedient Servants,

JONATHAN LEES,
London Missionary Society.

WILLIAM N. HALL,
Methodist Missionary Society.

To W. H. LAY, Esq.,
  H. B. M. Consul.

No. 44.

TIENTSIN.

(From our Correspondent.)

COUNT Rochechouart came by boat from Tungchow escorted by the prefect till near Tientsin, when Chung-how sent a guard. The French flag was carried all the way.

Two gentlemen wishing to go on business to the French side got a mounted mandarin from Chung-How to accompany them. They were taken a back way and not over-pleasantly received by the people.

The French were to have removed their dead from the British to the French cemetery, but Chung-How recommended some delay as things were not yet quite quiet.

The Chinese had a report that the *Survonada* had arrived at Taku with 1,000 French troops; the result was a panic in the city, the rich people flying to Pekin and elsewhere, and 60 passengers were booked by the *Chihli*.

Mr. Lay H. B. M. consul sent a circular on the 20th to the British residents stating that the city is now considered safe for British subjects to visit on their usual business, but earnestly cautioning them to avoid all reference to the past, and neither by word nor by look to give any offence to the Chinese. The notification is believed to be still premature.

Tseng-kwo-fan has paid a visit to count Rochechouart, not however until he was reminded of his duty. Tseng called at Mr. Lay's while Rochechouart happened to be there, but the latter declined to adopt Tseng's suggestion to consider the visit as paid to him. When the interview did come off, it was not particularly pleasant; Tseng-kwo-fan in excusing the people for their rudeness, remarked they would know better how to behave themselves in three years' time, hinting, it is supposed, at their military training. It is reported that when Rochechouart openly taxed Tseng-kwo-fan with the current rumours to the effect that he himself instigated the massacre the Vice-roy vehemently denied the fact.

No. 45.

THE CAUSES OF THE RECENT OUTBREAK.

TIENTSIN, 20*th July* 1870.

To the Editor of the

SHANGHAI EVENING COURIER.

SIR,—That the massacre at Tientsin, and the outrages which preceded it in other parts of the Empire are in some way connected, can hardly be questioned by any one well acquainted with these matters, and who is conversant also with the state of feeling and modes of expression common among the people.

That these acts of violence and bloodshed, with which, thanks to the criminal apathy of civilised governments, we have become too sadly familiar in China, and which will still not have reached their climax unless the innocent blood now shed should rouse the spirit which once made 'Civis Romanus sum' a word of power even upon an Englishman's lips:—I say, that these outrages are not simply the work of the people, and proofs, as we are so often told, of their bitter and invincible hostility to us, is also beginning to be understood both here and in Europe. The fact may still be doubted by those who meet few except the officials and the literati, it will probably continue to be rigorously denied by those who take their inspirations from the yamêns, but it is true nevertheless, and should be stated and re-stated in all its naked simplicity and pregnant meaning. The *people, left to themselves,* are *friendly* to foreigners. Many amongst us, who have travelled extensively among them, and had numberless opportunities of meeting them, both in city and country, have enjoyed too many proofs of their kind and even hospitable spirit to doubt it. There *is no such thing* as an innate and national feeling of hatred to us. It is true that the *appearance* of such a feeling can be got up to order. Any man even moderately familiar with the structure of Chinese society, and above all, with the terrorism exercised by the yamêns, can easily understand this. Let the word go forth from their superiors, let libellous stories be set afloat respecting us, and—the real authors of the mischief keeping carefully in the back ground—the ignorant and misguided masses, among whom not a few of the so-called literati must be numbered, will rise in bitter hostility. But, with the exception of the dangerous classes, which abound in every country to the dread of good citizens,—the people are glad to be recalled to peace and order, and are unquestionably every year becoming more and more disposed to recognise and welcome intercourse with foreign nations, as helpful and even necessary to them. The foolish suggestion of a late writer in the "Cycle" that the introduction of machinery and especially of steamers may have helped to cause the Tientsin tragedy, is only another proof of the obtuseness of men of his class. It is notorious that in the north, at any rate, the influence of such innovations has been eminently and evidently good, and that numbers would deprecate their removal.

We are thus brought face to face with the fact that to the ruling classes, or more properly, to a considerable and powerful section of these, we are indebted for our repeated troubles, and for all the difficulties which impede the civilization and evangelisation of the country. And it is no small addition to the mortification which such a fact is fitted to inspire, that it is but yesterday that we were fighting in the interests of these very men, and that they are actually indebted to us for their continued possession of the power which they use so basely.

Still, it is perhaps possible that the present outrages have another origin.

It is possible that the riots at Yangchow, Nanking, and Hankow, and the murders in Tientsin, Formosa and Szechuen have been due to other influences. It is possible that the Chinese government is anxious to observe its treaty obligations, and can hardly be held responsible for these things. I say it is *possible*: whether the evidence already at our command points to such conclusions is another matter.

Now Sir, it appears to me, that if properly sustained at the present crisis, the public press may be able to render most important aid in eliciting the real significance of these events, and their probable bearing and it is to urge upon all who have any facilities for gaining accurate information to use those facilities to the utmost and to publish the facts so obtained, that I now write. It has hitherto been the fashion to represent insult and injuries to foreigners either as mere local riots, the expression of popular feeling, or, at most, as the work of over zealous anti-foreign officials whose conduct the government disapproved, but could with difficulty control. The extraordinary state of things now existing must give a rude shock to such theories. Events of great moment are occurring in such rapid succession as to be almost synchronous—have they, or have they not a common origin? Can we trace them to some one influence? How far are the circumstances and the antecedent and subsequent action of officials alike in each case?—This is a large question, and which to be adequately dealt with, will need a large induction of facts.

I would venture to suggest two lines of enquiry which may be pursued jointly. The one is founded upon the assumption that these occurrences are due simply to the hatred of the anti-foreign party throughout the empire, while the root of all the evil must be sought in the capital itself;—the other rests upon the fact that even foreign alliances have not yet succeeded in re-establishing the tottering dominion of the Manchus, and that it is quite conceivable that astute revolutionary leaders may be willing to use foreign bayonets to weaken the government they wish to overthrow. It would take too long to indicate how these two lines of enquiry should be prosecuted. But with regard to the first I may hint that it is reported—with what truth I know not.—

(a) That the leading members of the pro-foreign party in Peking are out of office.

(b) That there has been, singularly enough, a general issue of questionable proclamations throughout the empire having reference to kidnapping.

(c) That everywhere, the crime is now connected with foreigners.

(d) That, unless overawed by the immediate dread of consequences, as at Yentai and elsewhere, the conduct of the mandarins in reference to the feeling thus excited has been similar to that in Tientsin. Such points certainly deserve examination.

With regard to the second, it may be enough to remind you.—

(a) Of the large Mahomedan element in the population.

(b) Of the unity and evident organization which so remarkably characterise the sect.

(c) Of the successful insurrections in the Western provinces; and,

(d) Of the enormous advantage which the leaders of these movements would secure if they could embroil the Tartar government with some foreign power, and so compel it to draw off its forces from the contest with themselves.

It is only fair to add that this latter is the explanation most in favour with many intelligent natives who are friendly to foreigners. They strongly suspect the present troubles to be due to the action of Mahomedan agents. They found their opinion upon the facts just alluded to, and also upon the prominent part taken by local Mahomedans in the outrages here. The fact that all the kidnappers as yet executed in the north, are represented as Shantung men is moreover looked upon by some as indicating that the 'evil rumours' emanate from an organization having its head-quarters in that province. Additional significance may perhaps be given to this suggestion by the undoubted fact that the events of the fatal 21st June were the subject of popular converse—in short, foretold—in Shantung ten days before they took place. Hints like these may not be without value.

If asked for my own opinion, I should say 'Both influences may be at work.' It may be that able as he undoubtedly is, Tseng-

Kwo-Fan and his compeers are to some extent the unconscious tools of others. But it must be alike our interest and our duty to endeavour to arrive at the truth. And whatever be the origin of these atrocities, common sense demands that such decisive measures shall be at once taken to vindicate the sanctity of foreign life as shall convince both the rulers and people of China that it can no longer be taken with impunity. A Chinaman said to me only this morning "A few years ago no one durst touch a *dog* which was the property of a foreigner, now even the Christian ministers are killed, and no notice is taken of it, see what is the result." He was alluding to the murder of my late beloved colleague Mr. Williamson. Was he wrong in his deduction? Yours obediently,

JONATHAN LEES.

No. 46.

THE following translation, of a notification, issued by the Chinkiang taotai in connection with kidnapping, shews the state of feeling which has been prevailing in that neighbourhood and the measures taken to allay it.

Supposing the document to represent a fact, we cannot help thinking that like success would have crowned the efforts of officials in other quarters—had they acted with the same promptness as the taoutai of Chinkiang:

Shên, by imperial appointment military intendant of the Changchow, Chinkiang, T'üngchow and Haimên circuit, issues the following important proclamation.

The taotai having occasion to inquire into alleged cases of kidnappers committing robberies, and, relying on their numbers, beating people, sent orders to the che-fu and che-hsien to investigate the matter. A few day ago four men were apprehended in the western side of Tant'u district and brought before the magistrate. On examination however, they proved to be police in the employ of the foreign opium tax office (or guild) and in no way connected with the kidnappers, so on finding security they were immediately released.

Though at present quietness prevails throughout this entire circuit, the taotai fears some rascals may make a handle (of the kidnapping stories) to excite the populace and may seize innocent persons with a view to obtain the reward offered for the apprehension of kidnappers, thus creating disturbances. This proclamation is therefore issued, warning all to attend to their own business and forbidding any one to circulate rumours or seize innocent persons or cause them inconvenience.

Let each obey with trembling. An important and special proclamation.

T'ung-Chih, 9 year 6 moon 23rd day.

No. 47.

A SPECIAL correspondent writes :—

TIENTSIN, 26th July, 1870.

The following news I believe to be reliable.

Nine bravo-chiefs have been arrested by Tsêng-Kwo-Fan, without the help of soldiers, by men sent by the new taotai, che-fu and che-hsien. Four of them are from the east side of the river (where the salt depots are,) the names of three being Ho-Urh, Ho-Sze and Hao-Pa. The other five are from the bad neighbourhood between the northern boat-bridge (on the Peking road) and the Ku-i-chieh (High street).

My Chinese informants assert that the che-fu and che-hsien have not run away: they are said to be in custody, and about to be sent in chains to Peking to be delivered to the Hsing-pu (Board of Punishments) for trial. This would be a pretty severe proceeding according to Chinese ideas, as officials do not generally come under the Hsingpu but under the Lipu (Board of Administration) for disciplinary punishment. But I do not think the French will be satisfied with this.

As to the famous Cheng-Kwo-Jui's (or Cheng-Kwo-Shwai's) present whereabouts I have been able to ascertain nothing. He is a man of great note in China and his hostility to foreigners is admitted by all my Chinese acquaintances. An English missionary told me yesterday that he had heard from some of his people that the Chinese on the French Consulate side of the river had raised a great talk about two Europeans having come there in chairs, remarking : "Only look, these foreigners think they can come here again, but we will do for them yet." When we visited Tientsin city last Sunday, the looks of the people certainly did not betray fear.

Every now and then a single Chinaman would step boldly up to my chair and stare at me with a look which said: "you are not afraid to come amongst us again. Don't think we are afraid of you."

I have always been convinced that two deep-rooted Chinese superstitions are mixed up with the present troubles.

1. That there is a change either for better or worse in the affairs of States every 10 years. In Chinese novels, when soothsayers prophesy any great disaster or reverse, and are asked: When will this take place, the invariable answer is: Ten is the full number. Before 10 years have fully elapsed this thing will happen, And my teacher invariably remarked on reading this *"yu-li, yu-li*—that's reasonable." The last war with China was *ten* years ago. By the way; 21st June this year fell on the 23rd day of the 5th moon. The 23rd of the 5th moon 1860 corresponded with our 11th July. Did anything happen on the 11th July 1860 which the Chinese would have particular reason to resent?

2. In Chinese chronology *three* cycles of 60 years form *one* large epoch of time. According to Chinese ideas, during the first cycle disorder and disasters are common; the second cycle is the period of glory for the Empire; in the third cycle its fortune decays again. The Taiping rebellion and the wars with the western Powers took place during the first cycle, some 3 or 4 years since we entered on the second cycle, and China begins consequently to recover her ancient strength. I learned the above from my teacher in 1858 when nobody anticipated what has recently occurred.

No. 48.

TIENTSIN.

(From our Correspondent.)

July 20th, 1870.

I have no connected narrative to you;—mere jottings of rumours and reasonings. On the first news of the massacre reaching Peking, it is said that the Ministers wrote to the Tsungli-yamên that they would bring in troops: they were implored not to do so, and a guarantee given that all would be settled, &c.; so they promised that no troops should be landed. Rochechouart, it is said, considers

Chung-How not guilty even of apathy. It is said that both mandarins and troops refused to obey his orders, so that he was powerless. Supposing this pretty story to be true what a nice state of things in China does it disclose! Here has been a man among us for the last ten years, believed to be supreme and absolute, and the only one here who had the power of life and death. He has not unfrequently exercised his power, as in the Shantung missionary affair, when a proclamation from him quieted everything. But here when so many lives are dependent on his action, he takes no action; does not even use the common courtesy to reply to the British consul's repeated despatches, bringing the state of affairs to his notice. And now when all is over, for the present, he alleges he was powerless to act,—powerless even it would seem to give any information respecting the storm that was brewing. On the following day (22nd June) he offered to send down to the foreign Settlement for our *protection* 600 of the same troops, who on the previous day had refused to obey him! Had the poor man lost his senses, as well as his command over his subordinates and soldiers; or is the whole of it a pretty story which his friends are concocting on his behalf?

In further extenuation of Chung-How Rochechouart is reported to have said that he had a letter from Fontanier written only half-an hour before the massacre, and that judging from it, M. Fontanier did not seem to fully apprehend the danger he was in. It would have been very wonderful if he had done so. There is a rumour also that Chung-How and Tsêng-Kwo-Fan are not on friendly terms. It is said that lots of troops are on their way to Tientsin and Taku and that for some days small parties of soldiers have been entering Tientsin. Large quantities of ammunition are also being collected, the last addition being 1,000 stand of arms per *Nanzing* from Shanghai.

23rd.—I send you an official report of the condition in which some Chinese Catholic converts were found who, at the request of the French minister, were brought alongside the *Flamme* from the mandarin's prison to which they had been consigned after the massacre. The description cannot fail to shock your readers, and make even the female portion of them wish to arm against such cruel monsters. If accounts like these will not rouse to action foreign governments, what will do it? What a farce to send out our missionaries at the expense, not to say of many thousand pounds, but of their own lives and those of their converts, if no steps are to be taken to put an end to such barbarous cruelties. The authorities cannot say in this case, that it was the mob; for these converts have been all the time in the yamên of the che-hsien, a fact which must have been known to all the mandarins.

It is reported that Mr. Meadows has written to minister Low, complaining of Rochechouart's treatment of him in not receiving him when he called. Rumour also has it the Imperial Arsenal is stopped for a time. It is also said that at the interview with Tsêng-Kwo-Fan, Rochechouart told him he believed the affair to be a political one and that it was currently reported that Tsêng-Kwo-Fan was at the head of it. On hearing this, Tsêng-Kwo-Fan is said to have jumped off his seat, crying in great surprise "Me!!" and of course, utterly denying it. I believe Rochechouart is coming to the opinion that the Mahomedans had to do with the affair.

No. 49.

PEKING.

July 25th, 1870.

The following is an extract of a letter from Peking received this afternoon :—

"I had a warm discussion with——about Tientsin affairs. He said no Christian could speak as I had done; we should remember they are heathens, &c. I told him they considered themselves the polite and civilized people and us the barbarian and heathen: that we are now on the horns of a dilemma. If the French do nothing, life is no longer safe here without a large force; and in any case within a year we should have a repetition of the Tientsin massacre. Then if the French do anything, we are likewise in danger here, as you well say "like rats in a trap" (I did not say so to him;) we shall be taken as hostages. The French for our sakes and for the sake of their own people in the interval, must do nothing hurriedly and rashly. But it is of no use arguing with our peace at any price friends, who forget that their present privileges are owing to a war, which at that time they probably disavowed likewise. Diplomatists here will find an excuse for any enormity the Chinese may commit." *O tempora! O mores!* We are verily fallen on evil days. I would rather a thousand times trust myself to the Chinese pure and simple, than to our own officials, from whom in fact we get no support; we live simply on the sufferance of the Chinese. We are quietly told that if it had been only merchants and missionaries, England would probably have done nothing. But an English *Consul*, that certainly would be something different. The shepherds thus are everything; we poor sheep are nothing in the eye of the diplomatist. I was glad to see the matter ventilated in the *Evening Courier*. Meadows is a harmless biped, but it is from officials that our respective governments derive their information. Every fact that can be got hold of ought to be printed. Public opinion ought to be awakened and informed. Our representatives ought to get a rap over the fingers for their ignorance and indifference. They made up their mind hastily and won't change them now. This is thoroughly Chinese; never to diverge from the opinion first formed, but stick to it. It is for the 'busy bees' of the press to collect such a mass of information as cannot be gainsayed."

"Poor Meadows, how has the mighty fallen! He had better quit the country now. It is a pity that our position here prevents us from serving some folks in a similar way. But we have some hope in the power of an honest and well-informed press. I hope a tremendous feeling may be aroused at home. We must have Taku, Tientsin and Peking well protected this winter. People here with families have grave doubts about spending the winter here, unless something be done to give us some security. I believe many will move off. Rumours are rife here, and kidnappers are being apprehended. This is now a common epithet hurled at one in the street, and at the converts." 'There go the kidnappers.'

In a postscript the above correspondent adds: "Dr.———said to-day (strange for him!) that a thunder cloud might break over us any moment. He fears war I suppose."

The same gentlemen who went up to town ten days since, again visited it two days ago. On telling Chung-How that they were going he sent with them four mounted mandarins and one not mounted. When they got close to the narrow streets they were joined by ten soldiers, apparently as a guard; they seemed unarmed, but may have had their weapons under their loose clothes. The gentlemen did not wish them to go with them, but they said they had strict orders not to lose sight of them. Is this escort a sign of fear lest the people should rise afresh on foreigners? The Protestant converts report that when coming in from the country they saw a great many soldiers coming in towards Tientsin.

These converts have been of the greatest assistance to us in bringing information; without them we would have been greatly in the dark as to what was going on. I have not heard of a single convert having deserted his standard; and this speaks volumes for them, and for the labours of the missionaries during the last nine years in "the Tientsin Vineyard." The Catholics also both before and after their tortures stood up for the faith. With Ministers such as Wade, Low & Co., no ways desirous of information themselves, we should have been badly off, but for our missionaries and their converts.

Wade was expected here to-day, but I have not yet heard of his arrival. It was intended to have had a meeting to-day of the Ministers, Admirals, &c., &c. Rochechouart is reported as intending to return to Peking in a few days, to deliver, it is said, his ultimatum. Telegrams from England *via* Kiachta do not yet mention the massacre, but there is one announcing the death of Lord Clarendon.

The yamên has sent down to the French fathers 138 children, and have given them a building belonging to the Customs about a mile below the Settlement and close under the fort. They have been placed in charge of some women who were also saved. I have not yet heard of the female French converts having been given up, though no doubt they will be so soon. There are still a number of children missing, some of whom are known to have been stolen, and the missionaries know where some of them are.

A gentleman living in the city whose partner is at present absent writes:

"If I were alone I should certainly have all my valuables removed. Some of my servants up town are now in a greater funk than ever. And the prospect of a prompt and satisfactory settlement seems very far off; while if no decisive steps are taken soon, it surely won't be safe to remain here during the winter." Compare this with the extra guard to the two gentlemen, and consider what the result portends. The French officers still blame Rochechouart for his inaction, and seem to think he is in a great measure guided by the other ministers. If he has not the power to make the Chinese give up the heads of the three mandarins he named; viz: the che-fu, che-hsien and Chen-Kwo-Shwai, he has made a great mistake. The Chinese will not give them up; and to them it is nothing less than a declaration of war. The Chinese all this time are having the best of it. Their troops are concentrating around

Taku, and at the signal will take possession of both places and declare war themselves when they are ready. The Chinese won't trouble themselves much about Wheaton's International Law; it is only brought out when a foreign nation breaks the law; then comes forth the learning connected with it, and who so able to expound it as its worthy translator at Peking, the President of the college?

No. 50.

THE *Peking Gazette* of July 24th contains the following edicts in relation to the Tientsin massacre:—

Tsêng-Kwo-Fan and Chung-How memorialize Us reporting the main features of their inquiry into the outbreak at Tientsin. They state that having stringently investigated the question relating to drugging and kidnapping on the part of the Chistians; [it is found that] although Wang-Sang has indeed confessed having administered drugs to Wu-Lan-Siu, his confession has nevertheless alternated with denial, and there is moreover no actual evidence of instigation on the part of the mission. The hundred and fifty odd male and female children found at the Jen-Tsze-Tang all state that they were sent by their parents to the establishment in question to be brought up, and nothing in the shape of being kidnapped has taken place. As regards the matter of digging out the eyes and scooping away the heart, Tsêng-Kwo-Fan has himself, on his arrival at Tientsin, made the most careful inquiry, and the people have been unable to establish the authenticity of the charges. On inquiry being made in the city and neighbourhood of Tientsin, moreover, no cases have been ascertained of complaint being lodged with regard to missing children. The circumstances in this case resemble those in the provinces of Hunan and Kiangsi, at Yangchow, Tienmen, and Tamingfu and Kwangpingfu in Chihli, at all of which places missives and placards have been extensively made public in a variety of ways. At all these places respectively the difficulties have been terminated, but the truth or falsity of the missives and placards has never been placed in a proper light. The people of Tientsin, continually hearing the statements of these missives and placards, have given credence to them, and furthermore, owing to the circumstance that the doors of the foreign missionary establishment

were barred from one year's end to another and that underneath
the Cathedral (*Jen Tsze Tang*) there existed vaults, which were
intended to keep off damps and for the storage of coal,—as also
that sick persons undergoing treatment were detained within, and
that destitute people and those at the point of death were taken
in, they harboured suspicions of which they could not divest their
minds. It so happened in the fourth and fifth moons of this year
that the kidnapping of certain persons by means of drugs took place,
and the Mission was dragged into connection therewith. The
people saw the Consul Fontanier discharge his pistol at the officials,
and thereupon a clamour arose from ten thousand voices, and all
rose simultaneously. The truth is that the reports about scooping
out eyes and hearts, and putting individuals to a cruel death are
for the most part baseless calumnies, aud have no actual foundation whatever. Thus far the tenor of the Memorial.

In this matter We have repeatedly enjoined upon Tsêng-Kwo-
Fan to co-operate with Chung-How in taking action strictly in
accord with the principles of justice, and the said Viceroy with his
colleague now report to Us that these matters are all idle rumours.
The source of the suspicions aroused in the minds of the people of
Tientsin being clearly manifest in the eyes of all, if similar reports
and popular suspicions should arise at any localities in the Provinces,
it will be possible to some extent to dissipate them also. As regards
the drugging and kidnapping of individuals by evil-minded persons,
the penal enactments directed against this practice do not lack
severity, but it may be feared that through lapse of time the law
has become disregarded; and We command the Board of Punishments therefore, in all cases where malefactors of this class are
brought to trial, to pronounce a sentence of aggravated severity;
and henceforward throughout the Empire whenever criminals guilty
of drugging and kidnapping are apprehended, let the crime be
punished with additional severity in accordance with the decision
arrived at by the Board of Punishments, in order that murderous
destruction of life may be repressed. At the capital, as the chief
centre of good order, it is still more needful that evil-doers be
sought out and arrested; and We enjoin upon the commanders of
the metropolitan constabulary that constant efforts be directed to
this end, and that any offenders of this description be at once
apprehended and handed over to the Board of Punishments to be
dealt with severely. Respect this !

Tseng-Kwo-Fan memorializes Us stating that Chang-Kwang-

Tsao, prefect of Tientsin, and Liu-Kieh district magistrate of Tientsin, in dealing with the matter of the hostile collision between the people and the Christians, were neglectful as regards precaution before the affair took place, and, after it had occurred, shewed themselves further incapable of promptly apprehending the offenders, on which grounds he solicits that these two officials be stripped of their rank and subjected to punishment. We ordain hereupon that Chang-Kwang-Tsao and Liu-Kieh (the che-fu and che-hsien) be at once stripped of their rank and handed over to the Board of Punishment for adjudication of their offence. Let the Board take note hereof. Respect this!

No. 51.

WE are again able to present our readers with selections from a letter received by a gentleman from a friend at Peking.

PEKING, 20*th July*, 1870.

* * * * * * Cheng-kwo-Shwai is living in the Chinese city here. In the Peking Gazette of the 16th instant, we have the details of a kidnapping case *without comment*. But it is a most significant fact that of the numerous cases of that crime which are reported from *all* quarters at present, the compilers of the Gazette should at such a crisis as this select a case said to have occurred in the *Ha Ta men* (great street) where foreign Missionaries chiefly reside. The consequence is that whether the selection was made by moony, underling-led mandarins, or was the result of artful design, that Gazette has gone far to neutralise any effect the Edict No. 2 of a fortnight ago may have had towards discouraging the idea of the connection of foreigners with kidnapping.

The fruit of this I have myself slightly experienced, having been to-day called a *kidnapper* no less than four times in the street; and a friend was nearly involved in more serious consequences. He was passing along the street when a child accidently followed in his track, which being observed by the natives, they made a tumultuous rush to the child's rescue, believing he was being "led away" by the foreigners. For to the disturbed imaginations of an ignorant people, plied with mischievous rumours and proclamations, the sight near a foreign quarter, of a foreigner closely followed by a Chinese young person, is proof positive of a case of kidnapping. Yesterday a boy belonging to Mr. Edkins' mission was taken to the yamên as a kidnapper. Mr. Welmann went to watch the case. After a night's detention he was released, it being found that his crime had consisted in *playing* at kidnapping with another child in a mud puddle, with a basket of tea in his hand to represent the dreaded philtre!

A well known Englishman was accosted the other day by the soldiers on their camp-ground outside the west gate: "We are going to kill you" said they. "Why don't you begin then?" replied English pluck. It is probably not generally known that a week was allowed to elapse before the American consul at Tientsin sent an account of the massacre to his legation at Peking. In the interval a distinguished member of the legation elaborated the following exquisite bit of logic. "It could not be much of an affair when the French consul could get coolies to carry his chair to Chung-How's yamên." Of course it could not. For how could the consul go to the yamên, but in a chair? and how in a chair, if he could get no coolies? Therefore you have had no trouble at all. So be quiet, will you? "And when at length the *Courier* supplied him with the first account of the affair that could be had beyond what his *worthy* subordinate at Tientsin had sent, and a friend proferred him the paper, he replied: "I dont want to read any account of it; my mind is made up."

A. B. C. F. M. in answer to the U. S. legation (turned counsel for the murderers, for this time only) replied that a blow that only slashed their breast pocket could well stand over till the crying murder of the French had first been dealt with, and that they would *not* insult the dead by sending in a bill for soiled apparel and accoutrements even though ordered to do so. They would choose a *decent* time for that business. It is well understood by all free-born Americans that in reference to this matter they are to say nothing of "danger" or "defence" no matter how closely the knife may graze them. For the dear offender affected by St. Vitus's dance and "*is weak at the extremeties*," and sometimes cuts people's throats when he only meant to shave off their ears, and so is not responsible except for the actual cost of replacing the bloody shirt collars. And in every case where life has been taken the government will make the extraordinary concession of allowing the victims Christian burial, merely reserving to the mandarins an official digging up and inspection. Surely this should appease the loudest cry for reparation.

Who will quarrel with the missionaries because they refuse to tell how many cash they will take to settle the grosset outrage the nations of the West have ever received in the East? Quarrel with them! Let the people left living in Tientsin unite in thanking them, and let the English speaking people especially, join in thanking Mr. Consul Lay for his manly attitude on their behalf, *when they had no one else to look to.* The idea to which you drew my attention some time ago, that the French and the mandarins were at daggers drawn about the practical working of the Extra-territoriality doctrine in the interior of China, as to whether the jurisdiction over Catholic converts was vested in the priests, or in the mandarins—this idea gets confirmation from an old teacher here. In speaking of this last stroke of the mandarins against the French, he spontaneously spoke of the jurisdiction difficulty as the principal cause. At the same time he scouted the idea of its being the work of the mob or of the guilds, except as they were deliberately put in motion by the higher powers, und that for a definite purpose. The French alone have claimed special privileges for their converts; the French alone have been attacked. Let Protestants make similar pretensions and they will fall into similar troubles.

The murdered Sisters were, 2 Belgian, 2 Italian, 1 English, and the rest (4) French. These martyred ladies are China's true ambassadors to the powers and peoples of the West. Had I the ordering of their voyage, I would first send them through America, to lie in state for 7 days in the chamber where, three years ago, a deceived Congress rose to receive their ravishers and murderers. Thence under the escort of the slumbering thunders of the navies of Christendom, would I transport them to St. Stephen's Hall, sure that, not to speak of the womanly sympathies of the Sovereign Lady, the sight of them would awaken even in the pacific breasts of Gladstone and Bright, some scintillations of the chivalry of Cœur de Lion. And mid the tears and honours by which their progress would be thus delayed, I doubt not that by the time I ushered them into the Imperial presence of him, who has specially assumed the function of "nursing father" to their church, I should find the object of their embassy already accomplished, in the unanimous determination of the civilized world to erect in China a "perpetual memorial" of the utter wickedness of those by whose hands they died;—a token of the "everlasting remembrance" in which they shall be held; and to prevent the possibility of such outrages being renewed, by insisting on obtaining for a great, but degraded nation, the opportunity of having brought within their reach all the elevating influences of a living and progressive civilization.

I have heard that on or about the 17th instant, there was here something like what we would call at home a "Ministerial crisis" in which the anti-foreign party were within an ace of getting a dominant control of the government of the country. Whether the report that Prince Kung, after an "indisposition" of some months, is again about to resume his duties, has anything to do with this matter, I do not know; but the party of progressive tendencies are reported to be more firmly seated than they were five days ago, and the crisis of the moment is considered over. Whether their seat is secure enough to carry them through the excitement that would arise should France declare war, is another affair; and I confess that the bearings of the questions are beyond me. I do not know the moves. But I should expect any government that just tided over the crisis of a war-feeling, to succumb after war has been declared. But remember all the above is hearsay, and may be only a *speculation* of our "learning-mad" sinologues.

Perhaps you may have already heard that the French Chargé was last summer directed to demand the right of audience, and in case of refusal a special envoy would have been sent with an army to back him. This was *last summer*. But owing to the action, or non-action, of the British Government, jealously solicitous that everybody else should be smothered in the same Burlingame mire as themselves, it fell through. The above will perhaps shed some light on the probable action of France in the present altered circumstances.

No. 52.

(From our Correspondent.)

TIENTSIN, 28*th July*, 1870.

It is reported that Tsêng-Kwo-Fan has written a letter to Chung-How expressing in the strongest manner his belief that the missionaries were innocent of the charges laid against them, and that the magistrate were guilty in not restraining the outbreak. He had thoroughly investigated the matter and found it so. This rumour you will find agrees with what is said on the subject in the *Peking Gazette*. Tsêng is also reported to have written to Chung, that it was no wonder foreigners were annoyed with the Chinese on account of their numerous breaches of the Treaty regulations; but that as foreigners are men not devoid of sense, who come to trade here, it is to be hoped that matters may yet be settled, &c., &c.

It is also said that Tsêng has written to the Emperor to the effect that the French are implacable, and that there is no chance ef getting on with them, by any peaceable means, as they are evidently determined to have war. The Emperor's reply, it is said, has come holding Tsêng responsible for the situation.

Well-informed Chinese will have it that Tsêng-Kwo-Fan is at the bottom of all these troubles, and that he is fomenting the Mahomedan disturbances for his own purposes, having ulterior objects in view. Tsêng and Chung are not friendly, and Tsêng's letter to Chung is believed to be a blind. If the contents of the letter were Tsêng's true sentiments, they would show him to be a thoroughly honest, upright man. But it is almost impossible to follow these people through al their duplicities.

I hear that the *nine* men (some say only *four*) who were taken up the other day have since been released. The Chinese believe that at present, Tsêng durst not punish one of them; there is therefore little likelihood of their heads being given to Rochechouart.

A protestant convert,—a simple man, living 600 li from here, having heard that all his foreign teachers were killed, came all the way to enquire into the matter, and went to the house, in the city, of one of the native preachers. He was caught by the soldiers kicked, and cuffed, and told that they intended to kill all the Christians; but that as he was a simple countryman they would let him off for this time if he would promise to go away 100 li from Tientsin. He promised, and went away. This was three weeks ago, and it is only within the last three days that he has ventured to come back and give this report.

Some of the Chinese here are remarking on the recent importation of fire-arms said to have been sent up by an American who lately paid a visit to the North. They say that if any Chinaman did such a thing he would lose his head here, and they ask if there are many Americans who are so bad.   The same Chinese also show their acquintance with history to the extent of observing that the Americans have never done anything in fighting for the opening of China, but have left that to the English and the French, while they have not hesitated to take every advantage gained by those who did the fighting.   They remark also on the attitude taken at present by Mr. Low and Dr. Williams.   It is to be hoped the Americans will not forget the remarks of these Chinese, whether in their trading or diplomatic capacity.   The *Ashuelot* is now here, and should there be any fighting to do, no doubt her gallant crew will do what has been done by an American crew before:— remember that "blood is thicker than water," and help with a right good will.

An address of the foreign residents to Count Rochechouart is to be presented to-day.   I hear there was considerable excitement in the city again, yesterday, the braves being anxious to be led against foreigners in the Settlement.   They take periodical fits of this kind.   Their arms which were laid past for some days, are I am told, again worn openly in the streets.   Mr. Moules, a drill master here to to Chung-How's troops, a good simple man, has had great faith in the Chinese that they did not want to fight.   This morning a message wus sent him by the mandarins which has rather unsettled his mind on this point.   It was to the effect that he was not to come back to the drill-ground until he was sent for.   No drilling has taken place since the massacre, but Mr. Moules went over occasionally to see the troops.

The meeting of the Ministers and Admirals is said to have taken place yesterday.   I have not heard a whisper of what took place there; but I hear that Baron de Meritens, who is here, has said that this is the murder of Frenchmen, not of English, and will not be allowed to pass unpunished.   I hear the French Admiral with several officers and sailors have gone up to town this afternoon.   To reconoitre?

It is said that Chung-How was down here yesterday and that he was very unwell; care and anxiety being the cause of it.

29th.—I have had a talk with——.   He says a telegram has been received and that the orders are: wait a month for instructions. He feels sure that Taku and Tientsin will be occupied, and the North opened.   Some chance of the coal mines yet, and rail-roads too.

Wade is here. He still holds to his old opinion. Consul Lay inclines I believe to our view and is somewhat snubbed in consequence; but he his right nevertheless, and holds manfully to it.

Rochechouart and Meritens return to Peking on Wednesday. Instructions not expected for a month.

30th.—Messrs. Wade and Meadows were seen walking arm-in-arm on the Bund last night. They are old friends, the former having known the latter in his official capacity. The *Salamis* and *Ashuelot* leave here to-day. Their leaving is no doubt owing to the fact that the French can *do* nothing for a month, and the weather hear meanwhile is frightfully hot and *stormy*. I have lost three nights' sleep which is more than I ever did before, so I think it as well that the steamers should go at present. Nevertheless it is a fact that Wade does not take the interest he ought in these affairs. ——says they got down yesterday two men and several women, and have now they think got all the converts. These women were present when the Sisters were killed, and saw them *impaled alive;* their bodies cut open to see wheter they were virgin or not; their hands cut off, and thrown into the fire *while still alive.* The more one hears, the more horrible is the account of these most cruel transactions. I had heard of the impaling at first, but could not credit it. and therefore did not mention it. —— says that in a few days they will have all the news, and know everything about it He has on his journey heard of similar practices to those here, from Canton, Foochow and other places.

Yours truly, ————

No. 53.

THE NORTH.

A Gentleman favors us with the following extracts from his Peking letter :—

PEKING, 25*th July,* 1870.

Fresh excitement seems to have been caused here by the insertion in the *Gazette* of that case of kidnapping referred to in my last, and proclamations founded thereon have been circulated widely, though not generally placarded in the streets. These proclamations call on the people to "seize the kidnappers at sight" or as the natives say "let not the kidnappers still remain in the city." The interest we have in all this is that it is foreigners who are really aimed at over the shoulders of the alleged native kidnappers.

There are present here some of the "T'ou-Muh"=="heads and eyes" of the Tientsin massacre who are reported to be in the outer city close to where Cheng-kwo-Shwai is residing, where they are displaying as a trophy a table cloth clotted with blood and boasting of their exploits in connection with it. This they do openly, yet while the mandarins, and the foreign ministers who support them declare their desire to punish those who *are proved* to have taken part in the bloody ourage, no one seizes these men, or even cries shame on them! They also assert that the Tientsin magistrates guaranteed their safety, and promised them promotion if they managed the massacre successfully. All this might be treated as mere braggadocio were it not that their presence here is itself a proof of their confidence that no punishment will overtake their work at Tientsin. Contemporary with their arrival and, no doubt, as a consequence of it, new rumours have arisen of a design to destroy the Catholics establishment here for alleged complicity in child stealing. There are no doubt plenty of the "long knife in strong sleeve" bravos here in the Chinese and Tartar quarters, to carry out such a design, if the public sentiment can be lashed up to the requisite pitch of superstitions apprehension. The French have issued a proclamation declaring that such menaces must be aimed only at *them* as they alone here take care of children, and giving an utter denial to their alleged ill-treatment of children.

The country people are reported as arguing, that the massacre must have been an official affair, as no one has been punished for it, and drawing this practical inference: "let us therefore follow out the imperial will and kill all the Christians." The war party are said by the natives to be Tsêng-Kwo-Fan, Cheng-Kwo-Shwai, and Mao-Chang-Hsi, President of the Board of War, who was entrusted with Foreign Affairs just before Prince Kung was taken with the sudden "indisposition" which kept him six weeks in retirement. Some foreigners here believe that orders have been sent to Tsêng-Kwo-Fan to have the Tientsin city magistrates beheaded. Perhaps this course is thought safer than to bring them up here for punishment in the present state of public feeling; and such a stern act of justice may do something to repress the anti-foreign feeling here which is every day becoming more bitter. There is a rumour that the French are to be attacked on the 27th

A native assistant is fearfully excited by the threats of the troops just outside the east gate of the Tartar city who have been bragging of what they will do. A singular body of troops they truly are. With their uniforms on they are brave enough to attack defenceless women. Stripped of their uniforms they are cut-throat brigands along the river, such as murdered poor Williamson at midnight. But if one wishes to get a safe conduct from here to Tientsin they had better apply to Dr. Wells Williams. Miss Douw and Mrs. Bonny purpose going down to-morrow and, as I hear, applied to the American Minister for a pass. From their picnic at the hills Low and Williams replied "O yes, it is perfectly safe, perfectly safe! Therefore go to Tientsin." O'Brien generously offered to escort the ladies all the way. On the other hand Wade who leaves for Tientsin to-day dissuaded the ladies from going. Mark this difference between Wade and Williams.

Wade goes to Tientsin, not of course on so trifling an errand as to enquire into a mob riot, but "to make a call on the Admiral." He makes much the same figure now as he does in "Swinhoe's Compaign, 1860." Parkes would not have got into trouble if he had not listened to the blind confidence of our Sir Hugh Wheeler. "Brave enough in action, Sir, but very stupid before it."

The celebrated American mermaid here shows a strange alternation of symptoms. When some fresh piece of news makes war probable, he wriggles a little and shows that if men will fight these Chinese eels, he will try the dry land for a little and side with the men against the fish, though of course only as an interested spectator. But at every thing that promises that matters may, after all, be pleasantly arranged he *naps* again—; reverts into W. A. P., and though he has at present got so near shore that he draws only half an inch, his splash still shows fellow-feeling enough to satisfy his fishy constituents that he, after all, never meant to desert them.

It seems likely that Rochechouart's visit to Tientsin has quickened Tseng-Kwo-fan's Report which appears in to-day's (25th) Gazette. It is to the effect that there is not a shadow of a foundation for the stories injurious to the Catholics, and that as the che-fu and the che-hsien (Chang-Kwang-Tsa and Liu-Chieh) did not show proper diligence in repressing the disturbance, they should be stripped of rank and handed over to the Hsing-pu

(Board of Punishment) to be dealt with as they deserve. Possibly now some of the foreigners whose superstitious regard for the written character, Chinese or English, is so gross, will leave off maintaining that probably some children's bodies *were* found with hearts plucked away and eyes gouged out. Alas! it is not the Chinese alone who are stereotyped and fossilized. Cheng-Kwo-Shwai's motive is clearer to me now. He is no Mahomedan; but but he *is* the mandarin whom Rochechouart procured to be degraded on the Yangtse, last winter. Here then is an illustration of the wisdom of leaving such an implacable and influential enemy alive in a nominal disgrace, the renown of which causes him to be regarded with the veneration due to a martyr, instead of seeing the man's head off and his power of disseminating mischief and misery for ever at an end. All the Chinese here agree that Cheng-Kwo-Shwai for one *cannot* be touched, without creating war. All the better say I. Off with his head then, French Provost Marshal, and give him the due attendance of those mandarins whatever their rank who executed his bloody work, while they still kept up towards foreigners the same kitten and lamb-like demeanour as did our boys in Hongkong when they were conspiring to poison us. And when this act of justice has been done, we may begin to look for a regenerated China.

No. 54.

A MISTAKE.

To the Editor of the
    "SHANGHAI EVENING COURIER."

Sir,

Some people seem to imagine that the Chinese have only some particular hatred against Frenchmen, or at most against Catholic missionaries. This is a great mistake. Do you want a proof of it?—Here is a libel first printed in Hu-nan, and several times, reprinted in this province; the mandarins are very well acquainted with it; the title is *An appeal to the Hu-nan Province.* The first lines of it are:—"It is much to be regretted that bad prin-"ciples are daily spreading out like a devouring fire, and sound "ones swoon away into complete oblivion.

"Strangers are invading all around, people's hearts are provoked "at it. Just speak of those rebellious and barbarous Englishmen; "(英咭唎) their savage country is the sea shore, the head of "government is a woman, and their original race is half-man "half-brute. They are those whom our books call *naked worms*, and *men-fish*." (倮蟲鯤人).

The conclusion is:—

"Wherefore we all literati, husbandmen, tradesmen and so "forth, let us draw the sword against the common enemy; who- "ever does not come with us is a traitor, shamefully sold to "foreigners."

INVESTIGATOR.

No. 55.

TIENTSIN.

August 3rd, 1870.

This morning the bodies of the French who were murdered on 21st June were removed to the site of the old French Consulate in the city. The foreign community went up in two French steamers to attend the funeral ceremony, officials being in full uniform. Mass was said by the acting bishop, assisted by two priests; the graves sprinkled with holy water and incense burned over them. Orations were then delivered,—by the French minister, who spoke low; by the French Admiral, bold and warlike; by the Bishop, on religion; and by Mr. Wade, who more especially addressed his own countrymen. The addresses seem to have produced a profound sensation among those who heard them; Mr. Wade spoke with deep emotion, and has done himself much credit. We give the speeches below.

The mandarins mustered in force, Chung-How and all the local people being present. Soldiers guarded both banks of the river and of the Grand Canal, which were crowded with people.

Mow-chang-shi, a member of the Great Council and spokesman of the war, or anti-foreign, party is in Tientsin for the purpose of assisting Tseng-Kwo-fan who reports himself "sick."

Count Rochechouart stated, returning from the funeral to-day in the steamer, that the Central government had promised the heads of the mandarins he had asked for, and he thought the matter might be got over without fighting, though it would be wise to be prepared for everything.

No. 56.

COUNT ROCHECHOUART'S ADDRESS.

Gentlemen,—One in vain searches history to find occurrences so execrable as those of which this city was the scene on the 21st June last. Seventeen French subjects, twelve of them illfated women, were massacred—what do I say?—were cut to pieces, by a fanatical mob, who not content to kill and to destroy, wished, if possible, to add to the enormity of their crime by venting their fury on the dead bodies. My tongue refuses to recite the details of these horrors, but I cannot pass over in silence the sublime behaviour of the Sister Elizabeth. A crowd, vast, hideous, bloody, has already surrounded the Convent, beats in the gates, and prepares to glut its hatred; then does that saintly woman come forward to the front of her offices: "You wish to kill the Europeans, "she says; there are ten of us: my companions are in the Chapel "ready like me for the sacrifice; come then, but spare the Chinese "who surrounded us." Thus indeed it well became those women to die, whose charity, devotion and piety are known to all. Who among us, gentlemen, condemned to live away from our own country, far from the domestic hearth, has not been glad to experience in times of sickness, the care and the consolations of these holy ladies who seem to know only the sorrows of others. You have been good enough, in two addresses, to express to me the sympathy with which these noble victims have inspired you, and to pronounce deserved praises on the courage of our unfortunate Consul, who perhaps might have been able to save his life, but who preferred to die in the place where his duty called him. Thanks Gentlemen, for that sympathy; thanks also for that claim to unity with us which you make; in China foreigners are all one family.

The forwardness of Chinese authorities to be present at this sad ceremony, is to me a sure guarantee (at least I wish to believe it so) of the good faith of Prince Kung. When His Imperial Highness has written me "the guilty, whatever their rank, will be punished" it is impossible to forget these words after they have been written, and for myself in spite of sad forebodings I wish to believe them—for the interest of the Chinese Government which would not wish by a culpable leniency, to expose itself to the just resentment of a nation like France. In the presence of these still open graves, enclosing the friends, the colleagues of yesterday, full of the future and of health, and some of whom had known only the roses of life;—I feel emotion overpowering me and sobs stifling my voice. Farewell them, my friends; you have given us good examples to follow in the performance of our duty. May we be able like you to die without weakness, surrounded by regrets and regards.

No. 57.

ADDRESS OF THE ADMIRAL OF THE IMPERIAL NAVY.

Gentlemen,—Afflicting as may be the sad ceremony which has brought us together around these coffins, I congratulate myself that I am able to be present, and to say boldly on this the very theatre of the massacre, that my entire sympathy is for those who have been the innocent victims of it;—that my utter horror is for the sanguinary beasts who have been its instruments, and above all, for the wretches who have been its cowardly instigators.

These sentiments are shared by my brave comrades, the sailors of Great Britain and of the American Union, whom I thank for their kindness in joining us in this demonstration of our sad regrets—of our intense indignation.

The remains of these unfortunate victims of duty and of charity, still, gentlemen, call for justice. The forwardness of the Chinese government to render them the last honours should make us hope that, yielding to the counsels of reason and of justice, it will make haste to chastise the principal instigators and agents of this unexampled outrage, and to give by its firm decision, guarantees which have become indispensable to all the foreign communities without distinction.

I cannot believe that it will be so ill-disposed or advised as to refuse to chastise those who before God and man, are responsible for the blood shed; that it will cast itself violently back from the paths (of progress) on which it had entered; that it will give way to barbarism;—that it will wantonly summon against its multitudinous subjects innocent of this crime, foreign arms which have already proved so fatal to it.

But I can assure you that if, which God forbid, the terrible duty of chastisement is imposed on us by France, shuddering at the sight of one of her Consuls murdered, of her priests murdered, of her holy daughters, of all these defenceless women cowardly murdered, we shall know, my companions and I, to fulfill it, without cruelty, I hope, but with all the energy, and with all the severity which the failure to punish such a ghastly atrocity would demand.

No. 58.

ADDRESS OF M. THIERRY, APOSTOLIC PRO-VICAR, SUPERIOR OF THE PEKING MISSION.

Gentlemen,—In the addresses which you have just heard, the kindness of the Chargé d'Affaires and of the Admiral has led them to dwell especially on the horrible massacre of the Sisters of Charity. For us, gentlemen, their death cannot be regarded as a subject of sorrow. They and our lamented fellow-labourers have reaped in heaven what they had sown on earth; so far as they are concerned, their death is gain. Come to China with the hope of the Martyr, they have obtained their dearest wish;— to give their life for Christ.

Permit us rather to deplore with you the death of our much loved consul, M. Fontanier; defender of missionaries, protector of the Christian religion, he has died nobly at his post, for it and for us. Permit us also to join in the general grief in regard to M. Thomassin, come to China for the same object, with his young wife, and so prematurely elevated to universal affection and esteem.

It is these and the other Frenchmen fallen victims to the impious hatred of the Chinese against religion; it is these, gentlemen, who should be mourned over. For ours, no tears, no vengeance; the missionaries,—servants of the God of Peace; the Sisters, daughters of the charity of Jesus Christ, can do nothing but pardon their enemies and pray for God's mercy on their persecutors.

No. 59.

MR. WADE'S ADDRESS.

Mr. Wade said that he spoke only in answer to an appeal. It was scarcely necessary to assure those more directly interested in the sad spectacle at which they were assisting, of his own sympathy and that of his countrymen, of the sincerity of their compassion for the fate of their fellow-Christians, whom they were met to honor; in particular for the fate of the unfortunate Sisters of Charity. One of these was his countrywoman. He had seen her but a few months past at Peking, engaged in her charitable work. It was indeed fearful to think that women whose lives were thus devoted to the best of good works, should have fallen victims to brutal ignorance. They had been happily reminded by the Abbé Thierry that to the Sisters at least, to die as they had died "was gain." It was Mr. Wade's humble conviction that no one who succumbed in the honest discharge of duty would fail to gain a reward.

Beyond the necessary punishment he would not speak of vengeance. He would but add, what he believed and trusted, as he could not doubt, every Christian present wished, that out of this great calamity great good would be produced.

No. 60.

PEKING.

Our advices reach to the 19th.

Disquieting rumours had been still very prevalent, one was to the effect that the 25th July, was the day fixed by a band of cut-throats for exterminating the foreigners in Peking. This had been talked of for weeks previously; and it is supposed the Imperial Edict of the 24th, published in the *Courier* of August 4th, (and which appears in the *Daily News* this morning,) had been instrumental in preventing an outbreak. Mr. Wade had paid two visits to the yamen on behalf of the London Mission converts, 40 miles south of Peking, whose lives were endangered by the excited state of popular feeling, against Christians, which is much increased by the fact that no one has yet been punished for the Tientsin affairs, whence the people infer that the government approves of the massacre. The yamen promised Mr. Wade to send instructions to correct this idea.

The Tsungli yamen are believed to have received some message from Europe which has caused considerable activity among their members. Some of them were called up in the middle of the night of Monday 25th, and many officials of note attended the Imperial presentation next morning. On the 26th, the members of the yamen were running about the legations asking whether they should behead the fu and hsien of Tientsin. This awaking to the necessity of doing something to satisfy the demands of justice is certainly remarkable for its suddenness.

Cheng-Kwo-Shwai wished to leave Peking for Tientsin on the 26th, but was restrained by a brother of Prince Kung's. He is allowed no troops about him, and it is feared he might be unmanageable if he got to Tientsin.

Some of the Pekingese have a report that the natives of Tientsin are on the point of rebellion against the authorities, in consequence of their assent to the beheading of the "public-spirited" mandarins who managed the massacre. They say there is no "Tao-li" in Chinese killing Chinese, so long as there are foreigners to be killed. Anyhow it is a strange state of things, when Tsêng places his troops in the streets "to catch the assassins." However, Tsêng *did* ask the consuls not to be offended at his doing so. Mao-Chang-Hsi, President of the Board of War leaves for Tientsin on 28th, which means that the pro-war party have got the upper hand again. Tsêng-Kwo-Fan's report exculpating foreigners, is not relished by a large party in Peking; he is even suspected of having been bribed by the French to make the report he did. Rumours are that the French have no troops at all anywhere, or that it will take at least two months to bring them on the scene, while the anti-foreign party feel confident they can destroy them with ease, and exterminate all Christians. The numbering of each house in Peking is actually going on to see where there are Christians to be killed. One man, a Christian, who occupied part of a house and refused to buy a joss or burn incense, but instead said his prayers every night, was deserted by his neighbour, who was afraid to stay with him through the 25th July, in case the mandarins should take him also when they came to kill the Christian.

The two parties in the Great Council are believed to be divided as follows:—

Peace party—

Prince Kung	
Jui-Chang	} Manchus.
Wen Siang (off duty)	

War party—

Mow-Chang-Hsi	} Chinese.
Hsueh-Huan	
Pao-Chun	Chinese banner.
Chia-Chen	} Chinese.
Tan-Ting-Hsiang	
Wo	Manchu.

There may be some inaccuracies in the latter. Some fierce discussions have occurred among them lately. Mow-Chang-Hsi seems to be a fire-brand; calls Prince Kung "foreigner," and Tseng-Kwo-Fan and Chung-How "Catholics." He declares that the kidnapping charges against the Catholics are true, and goes to Tientsin to re-investigate. He is loud-mouthed in bragging that as the Coreans repulsed the French, it will be much easier for the Chinese to do so. It was Mow-Chang-Hsi who collared the French interpreter at the Tsungli yamen and challenged him to fight, or something very like it. On the whole it will be seen he is a tolerably dangerous man to entrust with the "investigation" and control of affairs at Tientsin. A respectable gentleman on hearing of his appointment observed " I guess the French will find now they have got one that will pay them back in their own coin for their *brow-beating* of the Chinese!"

The most absurd notions as to the impotency of France are current in Peking; and as might be expected it is reported and believed that Messrs. Wade and Rochechouart fled from the capital.

No. 61.

FUNERAL OF THE TIENTSIN VICTIMS.

TIENTSIN, *6th August*, 1870.

The event of the week has been the removal of the bodies of the French victims in the late massacre, to their final resting place, within the grounds of the former French Consulate. As your readers are aware, the corpses recovered subsequently to the terrible 21st of June, were taken charge of by H. B. M.'s Consul, W. H. Lay, Esq., who saw that they were properly coffined, and buried provisionally in the cemetery at Tszchulin. Not a few of our little community would have been pleased to hear that they were not to be again disturbed. Englishmen everywhere would have felt pride in learning that the honoured bones of these martyred victims of political fanaticism and bigotry, lay side by side with those of many of their own countrymen. But, doubtless for weighty reasons, our allies have judged it best to take another course. It seemed fitting that the scene of the outrage on their national honour should become, in some sense at least, memorable as the scene of its vindication. It was evident that the sacred duty to honour the memory of the faithful dead could be discharged nowhere so impressively, as upon the spot where some of them fell, and it was plainly a righteous, however severe and cutting a retribution, to require that the nation which had slain them should itself prepare their sepulchres and erect over their remains a monument which should to all coming time proclaim their innocence, and the perfidious cruelty of their murderers.

Yet granting all this, there were those who doubted whether the time had come for such a ceremonial. To say nothing of the extreme heat of the season, and the danger thence accruing from so early a removal of the bodies,—a danger which was probably overrated—it seemed scarcely possible at present to invest the obsequies with as much of pomp and circumstance as the occasion demanded, and as was unquestionably desirable, in order to produce a lasting beneficial impression upon the native mind. The conveyance of the dead in solemn procession, whether by land or by water, attended by a considerable military escort, and accompanied in its route through the teeming population of Tientsin by some of the highest officials in Empire, would have been a demonstration of incalculable value in days to come, and well worth a little delay. Besides, there was a little more important reason for such a course. In accordance with native custom, the burial of the dead is always the last act in such a drama as that which is now being enacted in this city. The judicial investigation, the punishment of the offenders, and the compensation of survivors, ought all to be secured before the silent, but eloquent, witnesses, who were the victims of the crime, are consigned to the darkness of the tomb. Otherwise the matter is considered to be at an end: justice will rarely be obtainable afterwards. It will be present in the remembrance of all that this was our own experience after the murder of the Rev. James Williamson last year. It was then found to be impossible to yield to the urgent entreaties of the native Christians, who knew the customs of their country, that his body should remain uuburied until the murderers had been secured. But the sequel proved that they were right, for to this day we have no proof that one honest effort was subsequently made to seize his murderers, and thus the lives of foreigners are felt to be of little value.

However, all these considerations were doubtless weighed by His Excellency the Count Rochechouart and his advisers, and we may safely leave the issue in their hands. His immediate return to Peking appears to have been the principal reason for the course taken. The presence of H. B. M.'s Chargé d'Affaires, and of tho English and French Admirals, doubtless appeared also to render the opportunity a suitable one for tho performance of those last sad rites, in which they, in common with all feeling Christian hearts, must have felt an overwhelming interest. Accordingly, on Tuesday the 2nd August the mournful preparations began. It was thought well to encase the strong coffins previously used in boxes of still greater strength and thickness. These were therefore provided by the native authorities, and sent down to the foreign cemetery at Tzechulin. The task of disinterment, the enclosure in these huge wooden shells, and their transportation to the river, must have been one of no ordinary difficulty. It proceeded all through the night, and the noise made by the large number of men employed reminded us only too vividly of the howling shouts, which but a few short weeks since, proclaimed the near presence of a bloodthirsty mob. When morning dawned there were still several bodies awaiting shipment, and, as the event proved, there were one or two which did not arrive at their destination in time for the ceremony. As they successively reached the jetty they were placed upon separate lighters, and sent up the river.

It was about 5 a. m. when your correspondent, in company with other residents found his way to the bund. It had been arranged that the French gun-boat *Aspic* should convey the Ministers and Naval and Consular staffs, while the *Scorpion* was kindly placed at the disposal of foreigners generally. Mr. Wade however, preferred to ride.

As we passed up the well-known banks of the river, the scene was sufficiently exciting. As usual, at this season, there was a considerable number of junks at anchor, and the deck of each was covered as soon as the steamers appeared, with groups of eager gazers. All were quiet enough, for of course, strict orders had been issued by the mandarins to prevent disturbance, and it would have been madness to act otherwise. I did not hear a single offensive word. But there was no mistaking the expression of many a face, and it would be hard to describe the sickened feeling with which one looked upon some of whose share in the late atrocities there could be no rational doubt. Nor was it remarkable that the number of these repulsive, hate-speaking countenances was greatest in those very districts upon the east of the river, where the bitterest feeling has prevailed throughout the whole of these troubles. The *Hwen-hsing-tsz* are there in great strength, and are the dread, not merely of foreigners, but of their more peaceable neighbours.

Visitors of Tientsin will recollect the open expanse of water at the point of junction of the Peiho and the Grand Canal. The two streams do not form an angle, but actually meet, their united stream then flowing at right angles to both of them towards the sea. The French consulate and cathedral occupied a commanding position, looking straight down the river. Upon the memorable 21st of June, the spectacle from this point must have been fearfully impressive. From this, the centre of the converging lines, the banks of all three streams are visible for a considerable distance, and they were then crowded, as far as the eye could reach, by countless thousands, while from every voice there rose the cry of "kill." But now, as we neared the neat stone bund, in front of the consulate, the banks were all but deserted. On one side, Chung-How's foreign-drilled troops were placed as guards, at intervals of two or three yards apart. On the other, Tsêng-Kwo-Fan's wild-looking spearmen, most of them probably old rebels, did similar duty. Here and there curious spectators were seen peering over a wall, or round some street corner, but they were urged back, and in no sense could it be said that the ceremonial was witnessed by the people.

There was a curious mingling of the foreign and Chinese formalities usual on such occasions. A number of mat-sheds were ranged upon the bund, and here, separated one from the other, lay the coffins. Each was covered with a large plain black pall, to which a white-cross was loosely attached. Close by the doorway stood a native hearse, gorgeous in green and gold embroidery; while scattered over the ground in groups, were numbers of the strange wild men and boys with their conical scarlet caps always seen at native funerals, each bearing some fantastic gaudy emblem.

The vessels were hardly moored before Chung-How and his brother officials appeared. They had probably been waiting some time. Their presence was not demanded, but they had been invited by the priests, and doubtless thought it best to put in an appearance. Their plain undress contrasted strongly with the brilliant uniforms of the foreign officials, and were the subject of some adverse comment; but it must not be forgotten that no Chinese would wear official robes at such a time, and that their dress was therefore in accordance with national usage. The only mandarin of rank absent was Tsêng-Kwo-Fan, who was reported to be sick.

On entering the consular garden, the arrangements in progress for carrying out the idea of a memorial were easily understood. The ground had been carefully levelled, and prepared for its new use by laying out a broad path from end to end. On either side of this path were the graves, large brick vaults, 13 in number, over which it is intended to place suitable stones, while at the further end stood a mat pavilion, to be replaced hereafter by the monument which shall tell to future ages the story of the tragedy. It was said that the general plan had been copied from the Jesuits' cemetery in Peking and that it would be completed in a similar manner.

After a few minutes delay, during which several of the bodies were deposited in the vaults, and other preliminaries adjusted, the religious portion of the ceremonial began. This was conducted, in the absence of the Bishop who is now at Rome, by M. Thierry, the Pro-Vicar Apostolic, assisted by two others and attended also by one or two natives, one of whom carried a large silver crucifix. At this moment, and while the fathers passed from grave to grave, incensing each in turn and chanting the service of their church, the *coup d'œil* was very striking. The open space with its gaping sepulchres, the glittering uniforms of the consular and naval officers, the more sober, but not less effective, robes of the ecclesiastics, the little group of eager and sympathising foreigners and curiously impassive Chinese, the singular native ornaments in the background, with the charred ruins of the cathedral towering over all, made up a scene, which, aided by the recollections filling the minds of all present, will never be forgotten.   The religious service over, those addresses were delivered by Comte Rochechouart, Admiral Dupré, M. Thierry and Mr. Wade, of which you are already in possession.

No. 62.

PEKING.

On the 25th July the English cemetery was visited by officials in the same way as the Protestant chapel before mentioned.   This also is attributed to over-anxiety of the authorities for the safety of foreigners.   The authorities are showing other signs of activity. A proclamation is issued offering rewards of 100 and 200 *teaou* to the informer and apprehender of the thieves who broke into Mrs. Wade's temple at the hills, the thief or thieves to be forgiven if they confess and bring back the goods.   There are now night watchmen to protect the foreigners.

Aug. 11th.—Messrs. Wade and Rochechouart returned, the former displeased with Tsêng-Kwo-Fan, which is important. Some think owing to the European war the Chinese may go on massacring.   I think we shall probably feel so uncomfortable here in a few months that all the ladies at least will move off.

The foreign-armed troops in Peking are being drilled, after the foreign style, by Chinese drill-masters taught in the Tientsin school.—[*Courier* Aug. 18th.]

No. 63.

THE MAHOMEDAN REBELLION.

The following report of the progress of this movement reached us from Peking.   The authority is a military commander in the Imperial service.

The Mahomedans are fighting and slaughtering fearfully in the west.   From a late arrival I hear of cities taken and put to the sword, soldiers and rebels sometimes forced to feed on their mules, and, when mule's flesh fails, to kill their adversaries or prisoners and eat them. For drink extremity drives them to even more disgusting expedients. Mutilations of the body are said to be fearfully prevalent. The rebels are eight-tenths Mahomedans, and two-tenths "Chang-maou-tsei." They are reported to have many foreign arms, and to number 300,000. They force into their ranks those who prefer that to death. They are making for the east and south-east, that is, advancing on Chihli, and the Imperialists have their hands full in keeping them at bay. Daily fights occur.—[*Courier* Aug. 18th.]

No. 64.

TIENTSIN.

August 10th, 1870.

ON Saturday night one of the men connected with the foreign missionaries who arrived from the country *viâ* Grand Canal, reports the banks crowded with soldiers bound to Tientsin. One of Li-Kung-Pao's runners was seen, and these men are said to be part of 15,000 of Li's troops.

Count Rochechouart and party left on Friday, Mr. Wade on Saturday, and Chung-How on Sunday, all for Peking. A gentleman who arrived here this morning from Peking passed the Count's party yesterday morning about half-way to Peking. They had taken five days to go 40 miles!!—by water. At the present moment on account of the heavy rain, the land route is said to be impassable. Possibly reminiscences of comfortable first-class carriages, and a speed of 40 miles *an hour* may have obtruded themselves on the European portion of these travelling parties. A few such journeys would do much to unsettle one's faith in the Anglo-Americo-Pekingese dogma that China is better without roads, at least "*for the present.*"

It is reported that Mr. J. A. T. Meadows has resigned his secretaryship of the Imperial Arsenal.

Count Rochechouart is believed to have given the Tsung-li yamên till August 31st to give up the three heads which he has demanded, failing which he will haul down his flag and leave the country.

The Chinese have it that Tsêng-Kwo-Fan is very wroth that the che-fu and che-hsien had not been forwarded sooner from Paoutingfu. The che-hsien is said to be missing and is nowhere to be found, which is probable enough; and if the che-fu is sent from Paoutingfu to Peking, he will doubtless make his escape also. Of course, no one here, native or foreigner, believes the officials will be given up or punished for the massacre. If the French are in earnest, as they are believed to be, war must follow; and the more promptly and vigorously it is prosecuted the less will the Chinese suffer, and the greater benefits they will derive from it. For our broken treaties we have only ourselves to blame. We made stipulations on paper, and relaxed them in practice, abandoning one concession after another to please the Chinese, and now they and we are suffering for it, and war alone can remedy the effects of our short-sightedness and folly. A joint occupation and just rule of the northern provinces for a few years would do more good to China than anything that has happened since the days of Confucius, and even of Yaou and Shun.

A mandarin who has a reputation for more than average truthfulness, states that a Council of war was lately held in Peking, and out of eighteen or twenty who were present, all voted for war except *two*, of whom Prince Kung was one. The mandarin remarked that if they knew as much about foreign troops as he did they would not be so rash.

Another, an ex-official, also considered to be a reliable man, says that Li-Hung-Chang's men have begun to arrive in the northern suburb; there are thirteen thousand of them he thinks. He says he knows war is determined on as the only possible course to be pursued, as the government will not give up their officials at the demand of foreigners. The government would consent to the banishment of the three persons whose execution is demanded, and behead any number of roughs, and replace all property and so forth; but the *execution* of the officials, *never*. He further states that *a general rising against foreigners is being planned throughout the Empire without distinction of nationality*. This is from a man who has no particular connection with foreigners, and no apparent interest or motive in advancing his views.

No. 65.

TSENG-KWO-FAN'S MEMORANDUM OF HIS INVESTIGATION INTO THE TIENTSIN MASSACRE.

Having been ordered by Imperial decree to repair to Tientsin and enquire thoroughly into the events of the 21st June, I have, up to the present time, arrived at the following conclusions regarding these sad occurrences.

The first of the disturbances lay in the circumstance that missionaries were accused of being implicated in the kidnappings perpetrated by bad men. To this must be added the various rumours about eyes dug out, and hearts torn out; it being pretended that a certain medicine was prepared from these ingredients. And these rumours did not only spread from one to the other among the simple and silly people, but even amongst the gentry and literati there were many who brought forward the same accusations with one voice. From these accumulated suspicions, openly expressed dissatisfaction arose, and amid the consequent excitement the great disaster happened.

It is therefore necessary in the first place to discriminate between truth and fabrication, in order to separate right from wrong and innocence from guilt, so that we may clearly show that a just settlement of the matter is our only aim. And we must especially keep in mind that wild rumours of this kind have been circulated not in Tientsin alone, but that formerly in Hunan also and Kiangsi, in Yangchow and Tienmen, and even in the province of Chihli, in the districts of Tamingfu and Kwangping, anonymous and inflammatory placards were posted about, in which it was maintained either that the missionaries stole children, or that they dug out the eye, and tore out the hearts of men, or that women and girls were seduced and polluted by them.

And although the disturbances excited by those accusations at the above mentioned places have been severally settled, still it has never been thoroughly investigated and clearly shown how far the imputations contained in these anonymous placards were well founded or not; and therefore it has been my principal care since my arrival at Tientsin to elucidate these points singly by careful examination and enquiry.

First, as to kidnapping being practised by Chinese Christians; it is true that Wang-San made a confession of this kind, but even he denies on the one day what he had confessed on the other, and his statements are not in accordance with those of his comrades. And certainly no proof has been obtainable of the complicity of the foreign missionaries themselves in these abductions of children. Further, I have repeatedly examined all the boys and girls, 150 in number, taken away from the Sisters of Mercy, and they unanimously maintain that they had been instructed there only in religious matters, that they had been brought to that Establishment spontaneously, by their parents, to be educated there, and that they had by no means been dragged there forcibly by kidnappers.

Second; with regard to the tearing out of eyes and hearts, this is a mere invention without the slightest foundation in reality. It would appear that during the 4th and 5th moons of this year (May and June) cases occurred of two or three children who had died in the Hospital being put into *one* coffin, which aroused the suspicions of the people. And the gates of the mission premises being closed the whole year, excited suspicion by its mysteriousness, and because the people could not explain to themselves what was going on inside, a sense of fearful curiosity took possession of them. In this way evil reports spread to all the four quarters of the earth, and ten thousand cries of uniform accusation went forth against the missionaries. But it would be vain to seek for any foundation of fact on which these spectre-accusations have been based—it would be like trying to catch with the hands the passing breeze, or to seize a shadow.

When, some days ago, I arrived at Tientsin the people crowded around and stopped my chair, and numberless petitions were presented to me. But when I had made the most careful enquiry to find out what the truth was as to the tearing out of eyes and hearts, there was not *one* who could adduce a single proof that such things had happened at all. And when I enquired within and without the city I found that very few children had been stolen at all, and these cases had almost all been duly investigated by the Courts. But from what source all these false rumours originated, I have not been able to ascertain. I have the intention now together with H. E. Chung-How to draw up a memorial to the Throne in which we will give a general outline of the state of affairs, so as to bring to an end all these various discussions.

Indeed, to murder children and to mutilate their dead bodies in order to prepare medicine from them, is a deed so horrible that even uncivilised wild tribes would be loath to do it. England and France are large countries beyond the seas. How could we suppose them capable of such inhuman crimes? Reason forbids us to think of any such thing even as possible.

It may not be denied that among the Chinese converts there may be bad men who kidnap children and do other bad things, covering themselves with the name of missionaries as with a talisman; but this can only impose on us the duty to punish those converts who are found guilty of lawlessness; and must not lead us to lay these things to the charge of the missionary establishments generally.

It is the aim of the Catholic religion to teach men to be virtuous, and the Emperor Kang-Hi long ago gave permission to spread this doctrine in his dominions. And the Hospitals of the Sisters of Mercy may be fairly compared with our own Foundling Hospitals, &c. The desire of the Sisters is to found asylums for the miserable and poor. Charity and mercy are their device; if therefore they are accused of abominable deeds, foreigners will be justly prompted to resentment and wrath.

It is my wish therefore, that the Emperor should promulgate an Edict in all the provinces of the Empire, openly declaring that the misdeeds laid to the charge of the missionaries in those anonymous placards are nothing but calumnies; so that the wrong done to foreigners by these slanders may be expiated, and the doubts of the Chinese people and literati may be dissolved, and that every man in the Empire may learn and know the true state of things. In this way it is hoped that the distrust existing at present between Chinese and foreigners may be terminated, and that the hatred and ill-will between our people and Christians may gradually disappear.

No. 66.

PROCLAMATION.

Ting, a member of the Board of War, an assistant-censor and Lieut.-governor of Kiangsoo issues the following proclamation.

A short time since the business people of Shanghai misled by rumours were in a great state of alarm; the futai, on the occasion, issued a proclamation clearly stating that he had examined and found that the Roman Catholics had never kidnapped persons for the purpose of scooping out their eyes, plucking out their heart and so forth; he also instructed the Intendant, Maritime Commissioner and District Magistrate to adopt severe measures to repress the excitement:—All which is on record.

After this the suspicions of the people were completely removed and their minds quieted, from which it is abundantly manifest that there was no intention on the part of the people to create a disturbance; it was entirely the work of certain vagabonds who fabricated a lot of groundless stories and thus excited the ignorant, silly populace.

The futai has had the honour to receive an Imperial Mandate, ordering him to proceed to Tientsin, to investigate and settle certain matters there, but will return ere many months. Ever bear in mind the truth that all mankind are brethren (lit. that all within the four seas are brethren), peacefully attend to your business occupations and do not give ear to groundless talk nor harbour suspicions and doubts. Should any evil persons make up reports and create disturbances they will be severely punished by the local officials: when this is done, we may expect an improvement in the public morals and the prevalence of tranquillity, for which the futai earnestly longs.

A special proclamation—7th moon, 15th day.

No. 67.

TIENTSIN.

August 13th, 1870.

Tsêng-Kwo-Fan is reported to have gone privately to Peking without the knowledge of his troops. This, however, needs confirmation. Mao has been notified as Chung-How's successor.

On hearing of the arrival of Li's troops, the Captain of the *Ashuelot* sent an express after some of his officers who were on their way to Peking. On their return they reported having seen great numbers of soldiers outside, and thirty brass guns. The American Consul was requested to obtain information about them, and was told by the authorities there were only 2,500 troops.

At the Powder mills nothing is going on. The erection of machinery has been stopped owing to the state of affairs. But for this, they would by this time have been making Powder.

About a week since it was reported that all the mandarins at Taku had left for Tientsin. It was explained that they had only come up to pay their respects to the Empress Dowager whose birth day it was. They had left at dead of night, and curiously enough brought their wives and families and portable property with them! The troops thus deserted became uneasy; a messenger was sent down to report the circumstance, but found no one to report to. The officers have been made to return to their posts.

No. 68.

PEKING.

August 3rd, 1870.

It was reported that the government was impressing carts to convey foreign-drilled troops to Tientsin. The natives say the fight will begin about the middle of September. A Protestant mission chapel outside the Ping-Tze-Men was, about midnight of August 1st, assailed by Chinese soldiers searching for foreigners. The commanding officer explained that he did so in obedience to orders received from the Ti-tu's yamên. On investigation the explanation given was that the search was with a view to the foreigners' safety!

The example of Mr. Hart in withdrawing his family from Peking is about to be followed by three others, and more are likely to follow. Very severe remarks are made about Mr. Low who has been at the hills with his family ever since the massacre. Mr. Wade has never been there more than 48 hours at a time.

Cheng-Kwo-Shwai is reported to have gone to Tientsin about the 30th July and mischief is expected. The officers of the *Ashuelot* proceeding to Peking in carts, strayed close to the "Nanhai-tze" (South Park) a dangerous locality for foreigners to approach at present, owing to the number of soldiers stationed there. Everything indicates that the apprehension felt by almost every one is only too well founded.

We hear that news has come from Nanking that the Vice-roy Ma has been stabbed by an assassin and lies in a very dangerous

state. One of the numerous host of students now attending the
the triennial examinations is spoken of as the perpetrator of the
deed; and his motive is believed to have been resentment against
Ma's conduct in repressing the Nanking tumults of June last.—
[*Courier* Aug. 24th.]

No. 69.

TIENTSIN.

August 17th, 1870.

Li-Hung-Chang's advanced guard was seen entering Tientsin
to-day; a fortnight since Li was reported at Paoutingfoo where he
is supposed to be still. Ting is not expected to arrive for another
fortnight. 100,000 troops are believed to be now massed within
a day's journey of Tientsin. It is reported that Tsêng-Kwo-Fan
has been notified by the emperor that the three men demanded
by the French will not be given up, though some of the underlings are to be punished by the mandarins.

It is intended to man the Taku forts as soon as the French leave
this, and the defences are to be made stronger than ever before
their return.

The sale of the fans of which you have heard, and on which the
massacre was depicted, is said to have been prohibited by the new
che-fu; and the same official is likewise reported to have issued a
proclamation against spreading idle rumours.

19th.—News came yesterday from Peking that affairs were
likely to be settled amicably after all. Prince Kung's party having gained the ascendant, the emperor had authorized Kung to
settle with Rochechouart, the terms being that the che-fu and
che-hsien be given up at once, and Cheng-Kwo-Shwai *when they
can catch him*. Ching-Ling, as originally appointed, is to take up
his post as successor to Chung-How in deference to the wishes of
Tsêng-Kwo-Fan. Though this news is believed to come through
a French priest it is hardly credited, as Peking letters make no
mention of the circumstances.

Li-Hung-Chang is not yet here, although 500 of his troops have
arrived. He is said to have been brought on the scene to coun-
teract the manœuvres of Tsêng-Kwo-Fan. What does Ting come

for? and if by some accident these three powerful chiefs join their forces so near to the capital what is likely to be the fate of the reigning dynasty?

In this connection the following incident is significant. A Chinese Christian coming in from the country, when about 50 *li* from this took passage in a carrier cart. Shortly afterwards he was joined by a small mandarin, and a little later by a foot soldier, who entered into conversation together. The soldier said he had travelled 130 *li* that day, and was going express. The troops which had come from Ngan-Whui were pressing on as fast as possible. Tsêng-Kwo-Fan had sent for them to come in haste; these orders they received on 5th June, and they left Nganwhui in the same month, coming by way of Paoutingfoo. The soldier asked the mandarin the cause of the movement, and why they were sent for. The mandarin replied, Oh! I know all about it. You are going to *blockade the river*. If this story he correctly reported Tsêng-Kwo-Fan would appear to be, as is generally supposed, the prime mover in these troubles.

Mr. Hart has had several interviews with Tsêng-Kwo-Fan. At the last one Tsêng is reported to have said the custom in China is to give life for life, and they would give up twenty one assassins for the lives of the murdered French, but could not do more. A few days more will shew us the beginning of the end. The Chinese say Prince Kung has not the power to take the lives of the three mandarins; and that if he does, not a Manchu will be left alive.

It seems probable that foreigners will have to leave the North during the winter as unless affairs take a new turn it would be simple madness to stay here without troops on shore, since gunboats imbedded in the ice would be little protection to the settlement, and not much to the crews. They don't relish the idea themselves, without land troops. The *Ashuelot* has some 70 men on shore almost daily being put through their drill.

A Chinese told me to-day that Tsêng-Kwo-Fan has received promotion from Prince Kung and now ranks as a Prince. On the other hand a foreigner told me Tsêng was getting into disgrace and is to be removed.

The American Consul is reported to have asked Captain Taylor of the *Ashuelot* if he had any instructions from Peking. Captain T. replied in the negative. The Consul said things looked black and gloomy, and feared war would follow, adding "I have done my best to avoid it." Poor gentleman! he has done his best to bring it on.

No. 70.

We have now received official information of the death of Ma, Viceroy of the two Kiangs, who died at Nanking on the 23rd instant, eleven hours after having been stabbed in the groin by an assassin. Two ruffians were associated in committing the deed, though only one of them struck a blow. Both are from the province of Shantung. They were at once seized, and when examined declared that their reason for killing Ma was because the Viceroy had published a proclamation in regard to the Nganking and other riots, dictated by Rochechouart and containing a phrase indicating that the French were the equals of the Chinese nation.

Such is the official account of this tragic affair but as it is dated 24th August, it contains no particulars of what subsequent steps have been taken; except that foreign missionaries have been warned to leave Nanking for the present, and that serious disturbances may be apprehended.

But in addition to the above authentic information it is rumoured that one of the assassins had confessed that he was paid Tls. 5000, for agreeing to attempt the daring deed which has proved only too successful. One reason why the Chinese knew so little about the matter was that the Nanking authorities in sending secret news of the event to the Magistrates here, commanded them not to make it public, and so well did they keep their secret that when they were waited on by some foreign officials and asked expressly if they knew about Ma's death, they professed entire ignorance.

We observe from a telegram given in this morning's *Daily News* as having been addressed by the French Ambassador at St. Petersburgh to the French Minister of Foreign Affairs at Paris, that the extraordinary delay which has occurred in the arrival of telegrams *via* Kiachta, in reference to the Tientsin massacre is *to some extent* ascribed to storms and inundations destroying a considerable portion of the telegraph line. But the Ambassador adds that these physical causes (occurring with such suspicious seasonableness for the Chinese and so unseasonably for Europe) will not sufficiently account for the length of the delay. Altogether the matter excites reflections anything but pleasant, and seems fitted to commend submarine lines, as, on the whole, less exposed both to physical and to political influences.—[*Courier* 29th August.]

No. 71.

TIENTSIN.

August 23rd, 1870.

Affairs look blacker and darker than ever. An impression has arisen which I sincerely trust may be corrected by the result, that Rochechouart is blundering seriously. It is said that his *second ultimatum* expired on the 21st instant, but that he will continue the series without end. But the whole value of an *ultimatum* consists in its solemnity as a *final* utterance; and this is especially true in dealing with such a people as the Chinese. Cheng-Kwo-Shwai has gone south. Tiug futai has arrived. Li daily expected. No heads to be given up. The Chinese say they will clear us all out before the winter.

No. 72.

PEKING.

We hear from reliable sources that the Chinese Government has been seeking to make overtures to the Prussian Minister at Peking to form an alliance against France, which the latter indignantly refused. Rochechouart is acting independently of all the other ministers, he had received no instructions from his government and what his course would be on the expiration of his ultimatum nobody knew. The Chinese were waxing haughtier day by day, and seemed very willing to try their strength with the French. Messrs. Wade and Low were very uneasy regarding the aspect of affairs, and were expecting to find it expedient to send away all the ladies from the place.—[*Courier* 31st Aug.]

No. 73.

NINGPO.

August 30th, 1870.

A rumour was abroad yesterday at this port that a rising was intended upon all foreigners here; in consequence of this, the gun-boat lay at single anchor and under steam all night. As yet every-thing is quiet, but the absurd rumours of foreigners kidnapping Chinese are gaining ground every day, as you will see from the following, which was posted up in the city some little while back and is gaining credence amongst all classes of Chinese. The pla-card was seen by a foreigner who tore it down before a large and anxious crowd:—

"A Chinaman presented himself before the local authorities and stated that a foreigner coming along the streets had touched him upon the shoulder; as soon as he had done so, he found himself involuntarily following this foreigner, who led him away into a boat and took him alongside of a foreign ship. But as he found himself following the foreigner into his foreign ship, the spirit of his mother appeared to him and ordered him to throw himself overboard, which he did, and so escaped from evil influence and got home. When he appeared before the magistrate he was dripping wet."

This absurd story is believed by a large number of Chinese.

No. 74.

TIENTSIN.

August 25th, 1870.

The second period of Count Rochechouart's ultimatum expired on the 21st, but he has not hauled his flag down nor taken any decided step. His policy is becoming incomprehensible. The comprador class of Chinese confidently maintain that 'MONEY will settle the affair after all.'

The infamous Cheng-Kwo-Shwai, the Chinese Hercules whose feats are miraculous, would also seem to be somewhat ubiquitous. He is reported as staying with one of the military Wangs at the Anting gate, Peking, and at the same time as being in Tientsin under the guardian-ship of Tsêng-Kwo-Fan. The last report of him is that he has gone south to Shansi, Szechuen or Kansuh. After the massacre here he had a favourable audience of the Em-peror, but for state reasons was refused quarters with his friend, the seventh prince. These two afterwards met however and formed a plan for bringing down 10,000 flesh-eating Mongols from each of the 48 banners or tribes. The Mongols are reported to be actually coming, though not of course in such "round" numbers. Cheng-Kwo-Shwai has been accused of withholding the pay of his soldiers while in Szechuen. His accuser is in Peking waiting the action of the French, but Cheng-Kwo-Shwai is evidently too exalted a personage to be easily punished.

Childish as it appears to us, there is no doubt that the Chinese think the time has again come when they may try their strength with us. With foreign drilled troops and foreign arms, large and small, they imagine nothing further is required to make them a match for the foreigners. At least they are quite ready to try it. The common report is that as soon as the French leave this, the forts and river will be put in readiness to bar their entrance in the spring. No prudent man would remain here during the winter without a land force of 5,000 men. It would be sheer madness to send a small number. The Chinese know perfectly well that sooner or later the French will exact retribution for the outrages they have suffered, and they will therefore do all they can to get rid of all foreigners before winter so as to complete their preparations to resist the French on their return. This will entail the taking of the forts again as in 1860, with greater loss of life than then, and a stoppage of foreign trade for some time. Nothing can prevent this, but a sufficient body of foreign troops occupying the Taku forts before winter. This done, a light line of rails over the level country to Tientsin or even Peking would enable a small force to guard both places. Prudent people are sending home their families, while some are waiting a little longer. May they not be too late! The general feeling is one of uneasiness and distrust. Some of the Chinese officials indeed profess to desire peace, but with the order given at the camp at Peking—"keep your muskets clean, your powder dry, and be ready"—no confidence in their peaceful intentions can be felt. It is not for nothing that all the fighting men of the empire are being assembled in the north. Ting is now here; Li is daily expected; Cheng-Kwo-Shwai may be near at hand; Liew, a celebrated general is said to be here; Tso-Kung-Pun has been sent for from Shensi and some other distinguished managers of barbarians from other provinces. Tsêng-Kwo-Fan is reported to have taken about 50 of the fire brigade, 400 having escaped as soon as they heard what was going on. The story goes that 20 of the worst will be beheaded and 20 more banished, which would tally with what Tsêng-Kwo-Fan was reported to have said to Mr. Hart; "a life for a life: not that of the mandarin murderer, but of a brutal coolie in exchange for some of the noblest of the earth. I should hardly think *such* an exchange will satisfy the French or any other civilized nation. Twenty-seven coolies implicated in the murder of the Russians have been taken up; of these five have either confessed or are proved to have been guilty. The authorities seem now to be earnestly at work arresting these miserable wretches, and troops are being despatched in pursuit of those who have escaped. The *real* murderers, however, the mandarins, are all allowed to go at large. The old che-fu and che-hsien, the really guilty parties, go openly about the streets of Tientsin all this while. The first batch of coolies who were arrested turned on the mandarins, and roundly abused them for their treachery in arresting them for merely carrying out the orders given them by their captors. The later ones have also resented their incarceration, telling the mandarins to remember the foreigners at Taku and Yuen-ming-yuen. There is no doubt a bad feeling against the mandarins is being created by these proceedings.

One reason alleged for the unusual activity of the mandarins is the menacing attitude of the Mahomedan rebels. The mandarins fear to have the foreigners and the Mahomedans on their hands at the same time, and hope to propitiate the former by beheading some coolies and paying an indemnity.

Ting is by some reported to have brought a large army; others say only three persons, a secretary and two attendants accompany him.

Ching-Ling, successor to Chung-How, has arrived and taken over the seals from Mao. Ching has really been sick, and is so still.

The telegram of June 25th from this reporting the massacre was delayed 4 weeks by floods which tore down the telegraphic posts. This is from the Russian officials.

No. 75.

PEKING.

It is reported that all is quiet and likely to continue so during the winter, because the government have had so much trouble with the Tientsin massacre that they will try and prevent a repetition of it. In the city the police penetrate into every lane, and it would be difficult for any evil-disposed prefect to get up a riot like that at Tientsin without its becoming known to some of the numerous censors and place-hunters who might make capital out of reporting the plot. The legations and the admirals will also be likely to take measures for protection. On these grounds some of the foreigners in Peking consider themselves quite safe. The native Christians in the country however are not expected to enjoy the same immunity.

The Belgian minister leaves Peking soon. The report is again current that Chung-How goes to Paris, with a Chinaman who came back with Mr. Brown last year, and with Mr. Meadows and two young Frenchmen.

A French circus has arrived at Kalgan from home, after long and painful hardships.

A secret edict is out, laughing at the idea of giving up a mandarin to foreigners.

The defeat of the French in their diplomatic battle with the mandarins is understood to have given great satisfaction to Dr. Wells Williams.

Count Rochechouart's proceedings are severely criticised by foreigners. The Chinese officials are very insolent to him.— [*Courier* 1st Sept.]

No. 76.

THE NORTH-WESTERN REBELLION.

PÉKING, 25*th August*, 1870.

The following notes on the present position of affairs among the Shensi rebels, desultory as they are, make up a terrible picture of the state to which that and some parts of the neighbouring provinces have been reduced. My informant is a military mandarin who recently came on furlough to Peking with an escort of 500 soldiers from the Imperialist camp of supply in N.E. Shensi. He was twenty-four days on the journey.

The rebels are shut up in an island district formed by the splitting of the Yellow River in the extreme N.W. of Shensi in Ninghsiafu. They are shut in on all except the Kansuh side, whence they procure ample supplies both for themselves and their animals, of which each man has two or three. Foreign arms they obtain from the western Mahomedan cities, but no cannon; they are very plucky, and will kill as long as they have a knife left. The imperialists are expecting a supply of foreign arms and shells to arrive in September, but they will have little effect, for though the rebel camp is within range, the imperialist gunners will not be able to beat down the entrenchments.

My informant estimates the rebels at 459,000 men as follows:—

4,000 old Nienfei under their old leader, falsely reported to be dead, Chang-Tsung-Ya.

15,000 Szechuen men.

140,000 Kansuh men.

300,000 Shensi men under Ma-Ho-Loong, the latter being commander-in-chief.

The imperialists, some 300,000 men, are massed east and south of the rebel islands. The 4,000 foreign drilled troops are posted safe on the east side of the broad Yellow River. Li-Hung-Chang has his head-quarters at the capital of Shensi, 250 miles from the rebels, at which safe distance he directs the operations of the imperialists. When a fight takes place Mu-Fu-Shan always reports another victory! The pack mules with grain for the troops take twenty-six days to march across Shensi. My informant started with 300 mules and had only 70 when he reached his destination, the rest having been killed and eaten to piece out life by the way. The mules always consume half their load of grain on the way. Supplies for the troops are drawn from northern and eastern Shansi.

Northern Shensi is spoken of as depopulated. Solitary travellers are *killed and eaten*. The troops secure themselves from similar fate by always going in bands. Those of the inhabitants who have not been killed or forced into the rebel or Imperial hosts, have fled for safety to the charcoal pits among the hills, whence they prowl about like wild beasts for subsistence.

My informant expects that the rebels will hold their island position for two years yet, unless the foreign guns scare them out, which he does not expect. He says they have all the silver and gold of Kansuh and Shensi with them, melted down into solid masses the size of water kongs. A body of 4,000 imperialists have deserted, and hold possession of Yen-ngan-fu (north central Shensi), whence they make raids for subsistence; but they are quite overlooked as harmless; all the efforts of the imperialists being directed to keep the rebels from spreading northward of the Great Wall, following it eastward, and breaking into Shansi at its extreme N.W. point where the Great Wall abuts upon the Yellow River.

A great trade is done in captured and kidnapped children. Healthy ones are worth $2 a head. The soldiers sell them at a good profit in Shansi. My informant tried to bring two along with him, but one night they rose upon him, nearly killed him and made their escape homeward. This man claims that the imperialists hold Kansuh, but that seems inconsistent with his other statement that the rebels draw their supplies from that province. He ascribes the comparative lack of courage in the imperial troops, not to cowardice, but to their being worn down by terrible marches in sand up to the thighs and being barely fed, while the rebels have a jolly time of it and live on the fat of the land. The imperialists do not employ water carriage on the river, though it is navigable everywhere except at the mountain gorges. The country for 200 miles north of Tsinanfoo is still inhabited. Beyond that the opposing armies have swept it bare. A few months ago the rebels made a sortie round the Great Wall in Shensi, following its *nor'hern* side to Shansi, and getting into N.E. Shansi, they swept round the cities of Shensi homewards again, all the while pursued by the imperialists.

No. 77.

TIENTSIN.

August 31*st*, 1870.

For some days we have heard of the existence of a secret Edict, the contents of which as reported from memory by natives, made us eager to get a copy. This we have at last succeeded in doing, which I now send on to you, along with a translation executed with great care by an accomplished Chinese scholar.

As it is of the first importance that the evidence of its genuineness as an Imperial Edict should be satisfactory, I beg to submit the following, which has been corroborated by several native scholars, some of whom have special facilities for arriving at a correct opinion on the subject.

It arrived at Tientsin about a fortnight ago, and emanated simultaneously from a private individual, who had obtained a copy from a friend in a high official position at Peking, and from the yamên through the runners. It is the subject of common conversation among the official underlings. *There is not a native who does not believe it to be a genuine Imperial Edict.* The style is quite Imperial: and its existence for so long without any official repudiation has appeared to us as affording the strongest proof that it has really come from the throne. To forge such a document is a crime of the deepest dye, and liable to prompt and terrible punishment. It has not been placarded in the city and will certainly never appear in the *Peking Gaz tte.*

When it was pointed out that the document contained no reference to Cheng-Kwo-Shwai, although it was well known that his execution had been demanded, the immediate reply was: There has been no mention made whatever of Cheng-Kwo-Shwai, in *any* official document. The government will not even let his name appear as in any way connected with the massacre. This I think is a fact, and it is noteworthy.

The latest rumours which have a probability almost amounting to certainty, are:—The Viceroy of the two Kiangs is dead—died suddenly in the night. *Tsêng-Kwo-Fan is to succeed him.* Some of his troops have already left Tientsin, and it is said that Tsêng is to follow them promptly. Li-Hung-Chang is to succeed Tsêng-Kwo-Fan as Viceroy of Chihli. This is firmly believed by the people, but no one can give a rational explanation of what appears to be a degradation of Tsêng-Kwo-Fan.

For some days the city Magistrates have been most active in seizing the perpetrators of the tragedy of June 21st. There are now proclamations issued, stating that if "any one will guarantee their good conduct for the future, as well as certify to such good conduct in the past, in reference to persons now under arrest, they shall be at once liberated." The zeal of the officials has therefore been only of the most mercenary kind. Some of the biggest villains who took part in the massacre are known to be at large. I send you these rumours for what they are worth.

No. 78.

IMPERIAL EDICT.

Tsêng-Kwo-Fan and his colleagues having memorialized the throne to the effect, that the French Minister persists in his demands; and that he has petulantly returned to the capital to negotiate (the matters in dispute).

Rochechouart, with boundless arrogance and assumption, demands the execution of the Fu and the Hsien, a demand *ten thousand times to be rejected.*

We had previously by Edict commanded C'hien-Ting-Ming[*] to take Chang-Kwang-Tsao[†] and the rest[‡] and to bring them to Tientsin; we moreover instructed Tsêng-Kwo-Fan and his colleagues to obtain the depositions of the said Fu and Hsien, and in accordance therewith to return answer to the said ambassador (Rochechouart). We expected that with all speed this matter would be settled, (but) Rochechouart, since we have not followed his wishes, has in anger returned to the capital.[§]

At this crisis ourselves and foreigners are equally desirous of coming to an agreement (yet you) high officials of the foreign office are able of course with unalterable resolution strongly to oppose (all his) evil designs. Tsêng-Kwo-Fan and his colleagues must continue rigorously to seize, and speedily to punish all those arrogant, cruel and riotous men.[||] Respect this! 15th day of the 7th moon, Tung-chih.

---

[*] The Chief Judge of Chihli.
[†] The Foo (or Che-fu) of Tientsin.
[‡] The Che-hsien of Tientsin.
[§] The native interpretation of this is, that since the French Minister has returned to the capital displeased, the Che-fu and the Che-hsien need not be brought to Tientsin *i. e.* they may be set at liberty.
[||] The actual perpetrators of the crime.